MAGIC HUNTRESS

RENEE JOINER

Oshun
PUBLICATIONS
oshunpublications.com

Magic Huntress © Copyright 2021 by Renee Joiner

Hardcover ISBN: 978-1-956319-15-6

Paperback ISBN: 978-1-956319-03-3

Ebook ISBN: 978-1-950378-95-1

Audiobook ISBN: 978-1-956319-16-3

Book design by KDS Cover Concepts

Published by Oshun Publications

www.oshunpublications.com

JOIN MY NEWSLETTER

GET UPDATES, FREEBIES & GIVEAWAYS

RENEEJOINERAUTHOR.COM/NEWSLETTER

SINGLES BY RENEE

Singles
Tempest
Half Demon
Wanted Undead or Alive
My Soul to Reap
Gravetide
Vance and Vance
Cold Read
Witch's Justice
Ancestor's Magic
Strange Magic

PROLOGUE

I<small>N A TINY VILLAGE</small>, stood on stilts, on the bed of a slow-moving river, there was once a wise old man that had lived far beyond the natural will of the world. He had cheated death more times than there were fingers on his hands. The man lived alone in a small shack close to the middle of the river. He spent most of his days sitting on the edge of his veranda, swinging his feet off the sides so that they felt the cool water flow gently towards the sea. He was a warrior of sorts who had fought many battles before and lived to tell tales. He was a stern man who valued his privacy and a man of very few words, to say the least. He was tall and lean, his muscles strong and his skin the color of cooked rice, slightly brown but primarily pale. He had short gray hair that was bushy and unkempt, which matched his wild eyebrows that seemed to stick out in almost every direction. His eyes were the color of honey and, in the sunlight, looked like an amber-colored jewel that belonged on a rich woman's finger or around her neck.

He was not from those parts, but he had settled there after the great battle of the frozen glade, where he had seen things that he had wished he could forget. He had felt things in his soul that still made his skin crawl when he thought about it. He had never spoken of that time or that battle. And although he lived a quiet life of peace within nature, his mind was never still, and his heart was never happy.

One morning, the wise old man sat on the edge of his veranda, dropping his legs into the water and mending a fishing net that the current had ripped apart. The current had grown more unsettled and seemed to flow faster and harder than he had ever seen before. He knew that part of the river well. In all his years, he had never seen the waters flow in such a way as if the Earth was angry and frustrated at the men who inhabited her. He focused on his net in his hands and hummed softly to himself as he worked.

Suddenly, he heard something plop into the water from the veranda next to his. Looking up, he saw a young boy, not much older than 10, throwing pebbles into the flowing river. The boy saw the old man and smiled, his eyes lighting up as he did.

Then the boy did the most unbelievable thing. He took a few steps backward, then ran forwards as fast as he could, leaping into the air at the edge of his own veranda and landing quite hard in the old man's.

Although impressed by the young boy's bravery and strength, the old man maintained his neutral expression and demeanor, turning his attention back to mending his net.

"You are the wise old man," the young boy said excitedly. "I have looked for you for many days."

"Why is that?" asked the old man.

"I want to know the story of the Myxan and its powers."

The wise old man froze as though he had felt the touch of a ghost and stopped mending his nets. A serious countenance washed over his face, and his body became stiff and strong, as if he was preparing for a battle of some sort, ready to pounce at any moment. After a long moment of silence, the young boy spoke again.

"Please, wise old man. I just want to know if it will be able to save my mother. She is very ill," the boy's voice was shaky.

"The magic of the Myxan is lost. And if it was found, I would not use it on my own mother, for its power is all corrupting," the old man's voice was stern and deep.

"Please help me, wise old man." The boy was crying now. "There's no magic that can heal her. The healer in the village says she is going to die soon. If there's anything that can save her, I need to find it."

The wise old man stood up slowly and faced the young boy, and then he held out his hands and touched the boy's face kindly.

"Dear child," he said. "What do you know of the Myxan and its powers?"

"I know that it possesses the most powerful magic in the world. Magic that can save anyone and anything." The boy wiped his dirty face with his hands and looked up at the wise old man longingly.

The man looked down, closed his eyes, and shook his head.

"Come, child," He said, ushering the boy inside his home. "Let me tell you the truth about the great Myxan," He spoke through gritted teeth and with hate that seemed misplaced.

The young boy followed the wise old man into his home and sat on the floor in the middle of the room. Then he gratefully accepted a bowl of hot soup and a piece of bread as the man sat in a chair close to the fire that burnt, smoking on a pipe and puffing out dark clouds into the flames of the fire.

* * *

"At the beginning of time, when man and beast did not yet exist, and the Earth was covered only in beautiful trees and small magical creatures, a wall was built. The magical creatures that inhabited the world spent millions of years making the wall in preparation for man's time on Earth. The wall was not built of large, robust rocks that were sharp or uncut, but rather wonderful, glassy pebbles like those you might find lodged in the sand of a river bed. You see, the wall was built to separate the Northern and Southern lands. Although nobody quite knows who gave the instruction or why the magical folk of the time was dedicated to their cause. When the wall was completed, the good magical folk who had worked all that time tirelessly found themselves on the Southern side. Being too little to cross over the wall, they inhabited the Southern lands and lived peaceful lives since their duty was done. These magical creatures came to be known as the builders. But where there is good, there is also bad. It is the ultimate balance of the universe. You see, there cannot be light without darkness, and so darkness was allowed to grow.

"Over the wall, in the Northern lands, were creatures and majestic beasts surfaced. The lands were barren and scarce, and creatures fought to survive. Fathers ate their young, and mothers ate their mates, and that is how they lived for a long time. Surviving. Then men arrived in the Northern lands. They seemed to appear from thin air but inhabited the land as though it had belonged to them as a birthright of sorts. These men and women possessed no magical skill or talents, and they hunted the beasts and were-creatures, causing them to flee into the mountains and live in the shadows. There they faced starvation and great unhappiness.

"One day, a great leopard as large as a house, with eyes as red as blood and teeth as sharp as knives, came across the great wall of pebbles as he roamed about. He leaped gracefully over the wall and visited the Southern lands. The air seemed cleaner and fresher. The water was tastier and more refreshing. The grass was greener and lusher. But he knew nothing of those who lived there or their history, for he was new to this world, and his heart was still untainted. He was a great shape-shifter, and at will, he could transform into a human, with dark brown hair and eyes to match, a handsome face, and a solid and large body. And so, to enjoy the Southern lands, he shifted to his human form. He felt the grass beneath his toes and breathed deeply in the cool air. He ran his fingers along the soft petals of the flowers and smiled at the tiny creatures he came across. He felt happy and at peace for the first time in his life, and so he fell asleep, dreaming sweet dreams, underneath a large tree on the river's edge.

"When the shape-shifter woke, little creatures, all of which looked at him curiously, surrounded him. They had never seen a man sleeping naked under a tree, for the men and women in the Southern lands were always clothed. Around the same time that men appeared out of thin air in the Northern lands, so did they in the Southern, but these men were different. They possessed magical powers and skills. Kind and benevolent creatures took him to their homes, clothed him, and fed him well. Then they told him stories of the glorious pebble wall they had built for man's coming. The shape-shifter told the builders stories of his own home and the famine and unhappiness that seemed everlasting. When the sun began to set, the builders ushered the stranger back towards the wall and wished him well.

"In the Northern lands, the shape-shifter went back to his cave and told his family of the wonders across the wall. He told them of all the food and water he had found and the kind people who told him the story of how the wall came into existence. He told them of the humans with magical

powers and how they lived in harmony with the little creatures. He was sure, he said, that the little creatures would
show his own family the same kindness, and so he urged
them to follow him over the wall the next day. But when the
time came to cross over the wall, the shape-shifter and his
family could not. For the wall had grown twice its height
overnight, and although large and strong, the family of leop-
ards could not scale it.

"This angered the shape-shifter, for he was confident that
the little creatures had done this to prevent him from
coming back. He thought them selfish and cruel, and so, for
the first time, he felt hate. The hate grew in his heart, and
darkness grew in his soul, and so the magic that he possessed
grew darker as well. That morning, he retreated to his cave
in the mountain, and he began plotting his revenge on those
who called themselves the builders. They had abandoned
him and his people.

"In the years that followed, the great leopard shape-
shifter recruited all the magical creatures in the Northern
lands. Together, they plotted against the Southerners,
believing that they were the rightful rulers of the world and
that their powers, if put together, were undefeatable. They
trained for battle and practiced their magic. However, still,
the shape-shifter felt as though they were too weak, the hate
and darkness within him growing stronger every day until it
consumed completely him. He did not believe that they were
strong enough to take on the Southerners, especially their
magical skills and powers. But the shape-shifter was intelli-
gent and cunning and he would not accept defeat.

"He had watched the Southerners use their magical
powers to heal, and so one night, he approached a village of
man in the Northern lands, as a man. He walked through the
village, breathing in the air deeply and seeking the scent of
illness until he came upon a house where the candles still

burnt in the middle of the night. He knocked on the door, and a young man answered. The young man explained that his wife was ill and the healer in the village had told the family that she would die very soon. With that, the shape-shifter entered the house. He used a blade to slit the woman's wrist and drank her blood, claiming her soul as his own, and after that, he used his magic powers to cure her of her illness. With two souls in his body, his power doubled, and he felt unstoppable. And now that the woman's soul belonged to him, she could harness his powers through her own body as well. So, she accepted him as her leader and followed him. The woman's husband, feeling empty without his beloved, offered his soul to the shape-shifter as well. And so, the leopard-man possessed now three souls, and two mere humans could harness his dark powers through their bodies. They followed him with loyalty and were ever willing to do his work.

"As time went on, the shape-shifter recruited thousands of non-magical humans. He took their souls as his own, and they were able to harness a small amount of his power through their bodies. And with his army of beasts and newly magical humans, he tried his very best to break down the wall. Eventually, he and his followers succeeded. They stormed the Southern lands, causing havoc and chaos, and killed many innocents, claiming their souls as his own and growing more powerful than ever before.

"When that war was almost won, and the great dark shape-shifter had practically conquered the world, a group of witches and warlocks from the Southern lands created a spell to rid the world of his darkness. In the middle of the ultimate battle at the great pebble wall, a spell was cast to destroy the great shape-shifter. But, alas, his power was too great. He possessed too many souls to destroy all at once, so instead, his spirit was trapped in a box covered in sacred jewels and gems that were thought to have been touched by the Gods themselves. And his spirit lived in the box, causing all those he had touched to perish and his followers to crumble into ash. From that day, for thousands of years, the world was at peace once again. Although the great pebble wall was broken, the two worlds tried their hardest to coexist. However, it did not come easily or naturally.

"But somehow, the spirit of the dark shape-shifter was so strong that he became the box itself. Calling out to the weak and offering them magical solutions to their problems, if only they would allow a drop of their blood to fall into the box. A drop of blood which he used to possess their souls. And in return, they could harness his magical powers through their bodies. And so, the box disappeared from the world for a long time, spending time in the shadows with its carriers and protectors, all of whom had sold their souls to the shape-shifter. Legend has it that the exact pattern of spots on the back of the leopard's neck had magically appeared on the box's lid. It looked like five circles: One in the center and then four around it, each touching the middle circle once, like the four edges of a square."

* * *

FOR A LONG WHILE, the wise old man sat quietly, deep in thought, until the silence in the room was broken by the young boy's voice.

"How do you know all of this?" he asked.

"I was one of the warlocks that trapped the spirit of the dark shape-shifter in the box that is now known as the Myxan." Then the old man's voice went low, and he whispered, "It must be destroyed before the prophecy can come true."

"If you're a warlock, can you save my mother?" The boy's voice was shaky again as if he was about to cry.

The wise old man closed his eyes and dropped his head down. "What is your name, child?"

"Zak."

"Death is a part of life. It is the will of the universe. To go against the will of the universe is to go against your own heart and soul. For the universe is within all of us. The souls of those who go against the universe grow dark and unforgiving. Do you want to grow dark and unforgiving?" The wise old man turned the boy and looked deep into his eyes that were filled with tears.

The boy shook his head slowly and swallowed hard.

"I—" he began. "Can you teach me?"

"Teach you?"

"Teach me how to be like you."

"Some of us are born with magic in our blood. Others find magic. Some in their homes with their families. Some in their work. Some in the joy they find in swimming. You do not have magic in your blood, Zak, but you can find magic in your life. You just need to look hard enough. I'm afraid I have little to teach you."

"Please. I have nowhere else to go." Zak sniffled and wiped his face with his hands again.

The wise old man studied the young boy for a long time, looking deep into his eyes as though trying to find his soul. The boy was sad and alone, and he had little in this world.

"First, I will teach you how to fight."

* * *

THE NIGHT WAS dark and icy cold, like the sudden touch of death. Overpowering and numbing. In the absolute center of the forest, surrounded by thickets of tall green trees and full green bushes, there was a clearing of sorts. The ground in the clearing was flat and white; the last drops of dew frozen to the soil, creating a marble appearance. It also covered the trees surrounding the glade in snow, the leaves at the highest most points holding thick layers of white slush. At the same time, those towards the ground looked like glass sculptures in a glorious palace. There were hushed words exchanged in the glade that sometimes suddenly piqued in volume. It caused a leaf or two to drop to the ground, shattering and releasing an echo that seemed to last for minutes.

"It was the goat herder," a woman's voice said many in the group who nodded slowly, anger in their eyes shared the disgust in her words.

In that glade, the meeting of the Redgarde cult had been going on for just short of an hour. Still, their conversation went back and forth from the goat herder to their current predicament. There were dozens of people all dressed in long black coats with hoods that covered their heads and thick brown gloves that looked to be made of some sort of animal skin. They all wore black or brown boots and the clothes under their long robes were not visible. The Redgarde stood in a large circle surrounding a pedestal that sat at the core, about hip height and made of charcoal-colored stone. There was a mercury box on the pedestal, about the size of a loaf of bread, bejeweled with precious gems and stones and appearing to glow in contrast to the surrounding darkness and pedestal alike. On the lid of the box, there were no jewels or precious gems. Instead, the precious metal cover was engraved with an insignia of a circle placed dead center and four circles around it. Each touching the main circle only once, the place at which the circles met forming the corners of a square.

"There is nothing we can do about it now," an elderly man spoke next, stepping forward as he did and looking around at the members of the cult. "We were too eager to sacrifice our chosen ones and were careless in our security. These are lessons we must learn if we are to allow our beliefs to live on," he paused, and the entire crowd waited patiently for him to resume his speech. "Yes, the goat herder witnessed the blood sacrifice. We should have killed him immediately." The crowd buzzed in agreement. "Once again, we see that mercy does us no good. Now, our enemies are gathering their troops to cut us down. But let me remind you, brothers and sisters, our blood rituals have never failed us before." The crowd suddenly roared in agreement, excitement filling the air. "And they will not fail us now!"

The crowd cheered louder, and the old man triumphantly bowed, the mercury box glowing brighter as the voices of the cult echoed through the trees. Then their cheers died down as another man took center stage.

"Brothers and sisters," he began. "Even our youngest members have now mastered the dark magic within them." He nodded at two young men and a young lady who stood nearby. "They have conjured beasts and plagues, as well as paid tribute to the dark lords of magic by each sacrificing a virgin and bathing in their blood." The youngsters gleamed with pride as they listened to their praises being sung. "Now, it is time to welcome them into the lives of Redgarde. They must each let a drop of their own blood fall into the sacred Myxan, allowing their blood to bond with the dark magic it possesses."

The man stepped towards the youngsters with his arms held open. But before he could reach them, screams erupted from the forest around, and arrows of fire flew. Some members of the Redgarde cult screamed in agony as the flames ignited their bodies and sizzled their skin. Others ran in any direction they could manage while men with pitchforks and rusty swords charged at them, appearing from behind the trees.

"Freedom Fighters!" One of the cult members screamed and then slowly squatted down, placing both hands on the ground and bowing his head. He closed his eyes and took a deep breath, whispering words in some foreign tongue.

Just then, the ground shook underneath their feet. The roots of the trees broke through the frozen floor of the glade, piercing the hearts of the Freedom Fighters and lifting their lifeless bodies into the air. The snow on the tops of the trees melted to water and fell on the fires that burnt the bodies of the Redgarde, who had been hit with the flaming arrows. They recovered their strength and broke the thin shafts of arrows that stuck out of their bodies. Then, with little care for the arrowheads that were lodged in their flesh, they pounced into battle. The trees seemed to fight on the side of the Redgarde, their leaves swaying angrily and their trunks bending forcefully, hitting Freedom Fighters down to the ground.

The three young Redgarde, who had yet to take their vows and fully accept the dark magic of the Myxan, retreated into the forest, where they ran as fast as they could away from the glade and the battle. When they had run far enough away that the screams of the action could no longer be heard, they fell to the floor in exhaustion, breathing hard and fast.

"We have to go back," the young girl said. "They need our help."

"Are you insane?" asked the young boy with bright orange hair. "We're powerless. We haven't taken our vows yet. We'll be killed."

Just then, in quick succession, two arrows cut through the trees and landed in the chests of two of the young recruits. They died almost instantly, their bodies catching alight. The second young boy, who had yet to speak and the arrows missed altogether, gasped for air in shock as he watched his friends' lifeless bodies fall to the ground. Suddenly, a man stepped out from behind the bark of a large tree and looked down at the young boy. He wore brown trousers, a light-colored long-sleeve blouse underneath a thick black coat of animal hide, and dark brown boots. Although his face was kind and benevolent, there was a fire in his eyes that burnt almost as bright as the flames in which the Redgarde were burning.

"Get up," the man said. He held a drawn bow, ready to release another arrow, which was pointed at the young man's heart. "Tell me how to stop all this," he demanded.

* * *

BACK IN THE GLADE, the Redgarde were winning the battle, the dark magic on their side overpowering the Freedom Fighters' will. The villagers were all but defeated when the trees suddenly froze in the middle of the fight and retreated to their rightful places.

The Redgarde looked around at the trees retreating, confusion washing over their faces.

"No!" One of the Redgarde screamed. "What are you doing? Come back!" He shouted at the trees as they moved away from the glade.

"What's happening?" another Redgarde screamed.

Almost instinctively, the Redgarde turned to look at the pedestal that stood at the core of the glade. Many gasped in horror as they witnessed the sight before them. Some fell to their knees, crying for mercy, and others turned back to battle, using their sheer strength to fight off the Freedom Fighters. The Myxan was not on the pedestal.

"Nirmala!" One of the Redgarde shouted. "Find the Myxan. Kill whoever took it."

"Yes, Grand Master," Nirmala replied, grabbing the blade off the body of a dead Freedom Fighter and assessing her surroundings.

Just then, Nirmala saw a man running away from the battle, holding a bundle of cloth in his hands. He had a quiver that contained only two arrows on his back, and his bow was pulled over his left shoulder. He looked around at the scene before him, not noticing the girl studying him, and drew a blade from a sheath at his waist. Then he turned towards the forest and disappeared among the trees.

Nirmala ran towards where the man stood and entered the forest, leaving the battle behind. As she moved deeper into the forest, the air got slightly colder, and she pulled her cloak tightly across her chest. She reached out her hand, trying her hardest to wield the dark magic that she was so used to possessing, but it was no use. Her powers were gone. So were those of the rest of the Redgarde.

Slowly, she approached another area in the forest that seemed devoid of trees. It was not a glade or any other small clearing. It looked like a large sheet of glass, beautifully crystal clear, and through the sheet of glass, she could see water flowing rapidly.

"The glass river," she whispered to herself, shivering as she breathed in and out, her breath creating clouds before her.

"Drop the weapon." The voice came from behind her, and she felt the edge of a blade dig into her back. She released the weapon, allowing it to fall so suddenly that it startled her opponent.

She dropped and swept her leg behind her, forcing her opponent to the ground. The young man fell to the side with a thud, dropping the bundle in his hands but holding on tightly to his blade. Nirmala grabbed her own weapon and thrust her body forward, aiming for the man's heart, but he rolled quickly to his side and avoided the impact. He quickly found his feet, holding his blade out and slowly walking back towards the bundle.

"I don't want to hurt you," he said, squatting down to pick up the bundle.

"You cannot hurt me," Nirmala scoffed. Then she lunged forward, causing the man to lose his balance, falling on the glass river and skidding across, holding on tightly to the cloth. But it was no use.

The cloth, although still in the man's grip, was no longer wrapping anything at all. The bejeweled mercury box had slipped out and slid to the middle of the frozen river, shining brightly where it landed.

Nirmala ran towards the Myxan, trying her best not to lose her balance on the slippery ice. Before she reached the box, she felt a hand grip tightly on her ankle and pull her backward, causing her to fall hard on the ice. She flipped onto her back, struggling to breathe, and tilted her head towards the sacred box. The man had covered the box in the cloth again and was lifting it off the ground. With all the strength she could muster, Nirmala slowly rolled her body over and began crawling towards the man. His back was still towards her.

She grabbed both the man's ankles and yanked them towards her, forcing him to fall to his knees. They were both in the middle of the frozen river now; the water rushing underneath the clear glass lid. The man fell with such force that the surrounding ice cracked loudly, allowing the sounds of the rushing water to reach their ears. The Myxan fell onto the ice once more, and Nirmala and the man struggled, neither of them allowing the other to stand up completely.

Just then, two men appeared on the opposite bank of the river. They were dressed similarly to the man on the river, and each had an arrow drawn.

"Zak!" One man screamed. "Get down!" With that, he released his arrow.

The arrow pierced Nirmala's heart from the back. She gasped as it entered her body, then fell to the ice, lifeless, the blood streaming out of her wound pooling in little puddles on the glassy top of the river.

Zak was lying on his back, panting. He slowly got up and looked around for the bejeweled mercury box. Upon locating it, he made his way to its position. He reached down and picked up the box, then gasped and released it, his hands sizzling as if they had just held a scorching piece of iron. The box fell and bounced a little distance away, and the surrounding ice cracked loudly. Then suddenly, some of the ice gave way. Zak instinctively ran towards the riverbank, away from the rushing waters that would undoubtedly kill him instantly with their temperature. He watched as the piece of ice with the little bejeweled box broke away from the rest, and the weight of the box caused the slab to tilt, dropping the box into the gushing waters.

Zak breathed heavily, listening to the sound of the waters underneath the slabs of ice. He looked at his right hand, which was still burning fiercely. His eyes widened as the image that looked to be engraved in the palm of his hand. It was the same image that appeared on the lid of the bejeweled mercury box. Five circles: One in the center and four around it.

* * *

IN THE FOREST GLADE, the Redgarde fell to their knees, suddenly weakened by an unseen force. They looked thin and worn out, and they struggled to get back to their feet.

The Grand Master of the Redgarde looked around at his people falling to the ground. Some were struck with blades and pitchforks, and he watched as life slowly left their eyes. Others were beaten with wooden rods and their legs and hands tied with rope.

"Take them!" One of the Freedom Fighters screamed to the others. And with that, the battle was over, and the last of the Redgarde were captured.

In the village, the Redgarde prisoners sat quietly in their cages, whispering words in a language unknown to those parts. Zak walked towards a cage where a beautiful young woman sat, looking straight ahead with anger and disgust on her face. As he approached the woman, she whispered, like the others, in hushed tones that sounded sinister and uninviting and made the hairs on Zak's neck stick up.

"Don't get too close." A man put his hand on Zak's shoulder, much like a brother would. "So, you lost the box?"

"I had it in my hands—"

"Cloth," the man corrected him.

"That's what I meant. I had it in my cloth. I didn't touch it with my bare hands, I swear," Zak lied. "And then…" He dropped his gaze to the floor, his tone expressing his disappointment. "I just dropped it into the river, Jamar."

"It's okay, Zak," Jamar put each of his hands on Zak's shoulders and held his gaze. There was kindness and understanding in his eyes. "You did well. Without you, we wouldn't have caught the last of the Redgarde."

Zak nodded slowly.

"Come on, the execution is about to begin. The captain said all the fighters have to attend."

In the middle of the village, on a large wooden stage, the remaining 12 survivors of the Redgarde cult stood with their heads bowed down, all whispering in hushed tones. The executions were quick, and they hung each member without the opportunity to say much at all. When there was only one Redgarde left, the Grand Master of the cult, the captain of the Freedom Fighters, allowed him to speak for a moment before they hung him.

"Do you have anything to say, filth?" the captain spat.

"Only this," the Grand Master smiled a devilish look on his face. "You have all made a grave mistake. Life, as you all know it is soon to change. The prophecy is in play." He looked feverishly through the crowd and spotted Zak. Then he looked deep into the young man's eyes and laughed.

The concord inscribed will bring by false peace
As cozenage and truth engulfs all you know
The hate and the darkness will only increase
The heat of the great orb melting the snow
Dark magic shall burgeon and fill up the air
And the Cursed One will rise—

At that, the captain had decided that he had heard enough, and they hung the Grand Master without finishing his last words.

CHAPTER 1

BRENE WALKED into the bar and looked around. The place was deserted except for the bartender and a man in the back corner. A man who looked as though he was unconscious. She sauntered up to the bar and took a seat, sighing loudly. The bartender looked to be in his sixties, his hair almost entirely white and his skin settling in wrinkles on his face. His countenance was kind, and there was warmth in his eyes that Brene found comfort in.

"Beer, please," she said, smiling at the bartender and dropping her head down.

Brenley Tollis, who preferred to be known as Brene, was a slim and tall woman with skin the color of milk chocolate, pretty features, and eyes like a honey-glaze. Her hair, which was a darker brown color, curled tightly and set as an afro. She was wearing tight maroon leather pants and a black leather jacket with dark brown combat boots. Her motorcycle helmet, which she placed on the bar counter to her right, complemented her edgy look perfectly.

"Any reason a young and pretty girl like you is drinking away the day? It's not even noon yet," the bartender asked.

"So that I'm unconscious when my landlord asks for the rent this evening," she held her drink up and nodded before taking a sip, and the bartender chuckled.

When Brene was halfway through her beer, the TV mounted on the wall furthest to her came to life, and loud elevator music filled the otherwise silent bar.

"We interrupt this program to bring you an update on the Order's decision regarding the staffing and development of the new organization."

Brene sighed and turned her body slowly towards the image of a man in a tight dark blue suit. His hair was gelled back perfectly. Not a single strand out of place. His clean-shaven face stressed the deep blue of his eyes, making him look more youthful than he probably was.

"We have developed a new treaty between the non-magical human leaders and the Pannosus government. The Covenant of Assimilation, Integration, and Association, or C.A.I.A., aims to bridge the gap in understanding between humans and Pannosus so that we may live side-by-side in the days to come. The head of the Order, Supreme Pagzman Chahal of the Khonait Province, says that he believes this treaty will bring the long-awaited peace that they have worked so tirelessly to achieve."

Just then, an elderly man with pale, wrinkly skin and freckles that looked to be splashed across his face appeared on the screen. The hair on his head, although thin, was silver and so long that it covered his ears completely. From the part of his body that fits in the frame, it seemed like he was wearing a black cloak that was open in the front to expose a thick, bottle green sweater and a dark gray scarf tightly wrapped around his neck. On the left breast pocket of the sweater, there was a golden button pinned. A button that took the shape of a jaguar's head, its eyes narrowed and focused straight ahead. The elderly man spoke.

"My fellow Pannosus, I am here before you today to confirm the news of the treaty developed and the organization in charge of the changes that are soon to come. Humans can live in harmony with us, my dear companions. There is no need for them to fear our magic, or for us to fear their ignorance any longer. Millennia ago, when my and your great forefathers fought the spirit of the great shape-shifter and even later, when they found and destroyed the Myxan after The War of the Ancestors and the culling of the Redgarde, they secured our future in this world. They allowed us to not just survive but thrive, and the humans were part of that as well. The human—"

"Well, how do you do? Welcome back to DIY potions. I'm your host, Daxe the Decoction Diva. Today we're going to learn how to properly deworm your hogswiggle and thurntobs before making the perfect enchantment to increase the inside space in your handbag. You know, one of my aunts poured a little of this potion into her hand luggage bag. Never had to carry a suitcase again. In fact, once she pulled out an entire living room set from in there—"

"—and the new world jinx champion is—"

"It's okay. You can just turn it off," Brene chuckled.

"There's nothing good on TV these days," the bartender said. "That crap about us an' humans living together is nothing but hogwash." He was wiping some glasses as he spoke. "A pure fucking fallacy, if you ask me. The same people who wrote the peace accords clearly state that humans and Pannosus need to live apart suddenly want to come here and tell us it's time to move forward and forget the old days. They're the ones who wrote the laws of the days of old. They dictated how our grandfathers lived, and now they're saying that the way they lived was wrong. Then admit you made a fucking mistake. Don't create a whole new legal document just because you can. Fucking hypocrites."

"Yeah, I agree. Even if we end up living in peace for a little while, everyone would be on edge all the time. I can guarantee you that the smallest of things would set people off like you won't imagine. Like how all it takes is someone to sneeze a little louder than normal to get a drunken troll furious," Brene laughed. "It's not worth all the drama."

"So, you're not one of those activists who believe that humans and Pannosus should have equal rights and equal say in the running of the world?" The bartender raised his eyebrows as he looked at Brene, waiting for her response.

She thought a long while before saying, "No. I don't think there's such a thing as equality when it comes to humans and us. Don't get me wrong, I don't believe one race is better than the other or that one deserves more power," she sighed. "I guess, I just think…." Her mind drifted for a few moments. "I think about it this way. You and me, we look like humans. We smell like humans. We speak like humans. Heck, we even eat and pee like humans do. But we're not humans. Have you ever read the peace accords?"

She tilted her head and squinted her eyes at him.

He shook his head no.

"Well, in the peace accords, like any legal document, there are definitions at the beginning, okay? And the only difference, as per the definition, between the humans and us, is the magic that flows through our veins." As she said the last part, she slowed her speech, deepened her voice, opened her eyes wide, and held her hands up, wiggling her fingers in the bartender's direction. "The definitions are identical, except under Pannosus, it says two legs, two arms, one heart, consciousness, and cognition blah blah blah… and," she paused for effect. "Magical abilities. Those two little words make you Pannosus. And those two little words are the difference between living in the countryside surrounded by fresh air and nature, happily and freely, and living in villages.

Restricted to areas that have been ideally placed." She sipped her beer. "The question is, ideally placed for who? Us or the humans?"

The bartender chuckled as Brene gulped down the rest of her beer. "Passionate one, aren't you? The name's Deegan. I own the bar."

"Brene. A pleasure to make your acquaintance." She bowed her head slightly, bringing two fingers to her head and then sweeping them forward like a salute.

"Where are you from?" Deegan asked.

Brene sighed. "I've just come from a painful interview with the Order's recruitment team. Rejected," she shrugged. "They weren't particularly kind."

Deegan looked impressed and studied the girl closely. "I mean, where are you from in the world? Your accent. It's not local."

Brene blushed at her misunderstanding. "Oh. Well, I'm from the Sheffield Province. But it was destroyed by a band of Caeruleus. So, I moved here. I'm living in Eagle Rock Village now."

Brene clipped, clearly not wanting to speak more about the subject. Although Deegan seemed kind and understanding, he was a stranger that she had met at a bar. And from her years in the world, she had learned to trust nobody and assume the worst until proven otherwise.

A band of Caeruleus, rogue witches and warlocks who believed that they were above the law and refused to settle in villages or follow approved guidelines for the practice of magic, had destroyed Brene's home looking for her. Of that, she was sure. She couldn't help but feel responsible for the pain and torment they must have caused, but it was not her fault. She didn't choose to be who she was. She was simply born that way. That's why she needed to work for the Order. She needed to do something good. Something positive. Have an impact somehow. All she wanted to do was help, but every interview she attended seemed to end in the same way. Rejection. She had graduated at the top of her class from the Eagle Rock Academy of Enchantment and had received many job offers since. Excellent career prospects where she could use her magic to make people's lives just a little easier. But that wasn't what she wanted. She wanted to work for the Order. They could protect her.

Deegan' voice pulled her back to reality. "Those damned Caeruleus. I don't know why they have to cause havoc wherever they go. If you ask me, they should all be locked up." He was frowning, his white eyebrows clumping together like tiny hairy caterpillars. "So, what position did you apply for at the Order?" His voice was kinder now.

"It was a mage internship. The Order trains you for a year, and then if you do well, they absorb you into a permanent position. I was hoping to get into fieldwork. Become an agent for the Order."

"Big dreams. I like that," Deegan smiled. "Another beer?"

Brene nodded.

Just then, a bright red phone hanging off the wall behind the bar suddenly came to life, ringing loudly.

"Hello," Deegan answered, then silently listened to whoever was on the other end of the call. "What? What do you mean?"

After a few minutes of back and forth, Deegan angrily banged the phone on its receiver, grabbed a beer, and placed it in front of Brene.

"My server quit." He was furious. "One hour before peak time, and she quits. You know, it's so fucking hard to get good help these days. Everyone just wants those fancy jobs in those fancy organizations. In my day, being a server was a big deal. You had respect if you were a server." He shook his head.

Brene sipped her beer and thought for a long moment before speaking. "I don't know if you heard, but my interview at that big organization was a complete flop. I'm looking for a job if you know anyone who's hiring." She raised her brows, and they both chuckled.

"You mean it? You want to work here?" Deegan asked.

Brene nodded excitedly and took another sip of her beer. "I can start...." She looked at her watch, then back up at Deegan. "Immediately."

Deegan laughed. "Well, I know it's not the Order or anything, but you're hired. Welcome to Deegan' bar," he stretched out his hand for her to shake.

TWO WEEKS PASSED BY QUICKLY, and Brene had grown to instead enjoy her job as a server at Deegan' bar. Although most of the day was quiet, the rush hours were booming and loud, and the people were rough and unkempt. The bar's regulars were generous folk who tipped Brene generously and had grown on the young girl as well. Pannosus sailors, who seemed to communicate only with profanities as though other words did not exist. General workers from different parts of the village. Even some mages from the Eagle Rock branch of the Order drank at the bar sometimes and often offered Brene advice. In that little bar, Brene had felt a sense of belonging that she had been missing for most of her life.

"Can I get another beer, Brene?" a middle-aged sailor with a tattoo of an anchor on his neck shouted towards the bar.

It was a Thursday afternoon, and the usual crowd was shuffling in, almost like clockwork. The sailor sat at a table with two other men who were dressed the same as him. The three men wore white pants with a white sleeveless shirt that caused their enormous arms to stick out like sore thumbs.

One man had a blue scarf tied around his neck, and on the table, three sailor hats sat, one before each man.

"Sure thing, Deon," Brene shouted back at the man. "Frank? Jamar? Are you good?" The other two men nodded and smiled.

As the evening went on, the bar filled up, and by the time the other two servers had arrived, Brene had already attended to most of the crowd. By that time, there was a buzz in the air as friends excitedly recounted the happenings of their days, and drunken sailors complained loudly about their lives. People chatted merrily, and the scene was vibrant and enjoyable.

"Hey, Brene," a rather large man with bright red hair and a beard to match waved at her, and she waved back and smiled. "Working hard or hardly working?"

The two chuckled, and Brene made her way behind the bar where Deegan was busy wiping some scotch glasses, although his eyes were fixed on the TV.

When Brene got behind the bar, she turned to watch the TV, curious about what had captured Deegan's attention so intensely.

"—but authorities urge all Pannosus to remain calm during this time. There have so far been twelve solar flashes that have taken the space commission by surprise. Lead investigator from the National Space Commission, Dr. Kian Price, says that there had been no data to allow for them to expect or plan for the solar flashes. They were unpredictable and uncontrollable. Although there were few direct impacts of the flashes on the ground, satellite interruptions and radiation waves are expected and prepared for. In the event—"

"—for the final touches of your potion, you're going to want to use the hair of a loved one."

"You have the attention span of a squirrel, old man." Brene grabbed two glasses and used the beer tap to fill them.

"The news is nothing but an attempt to brainwash us all into believing that the Order and the rest of the revolutionists have our best interest at all." Deegan rolled his eyes. "It's all just one big political scam. You know, some people think the revolutionists didn't even find the Myxan after The War of the Ancestors. They lied that they destroyed it so that people wouldn't freak out. Then they created the Order to hide the truth and secretly search for the box to destroy it." He shrugged.

Brene chortled, "I'm sure that's not true."

"All I'm saying is maybe it's not a bad thing that those corrupt politicians didn't accept you into the Order. What's with the blonde hair?" he motioned towards her head.

"I thought it was time for a change. New job, new hair," she shrugged.

The truth is. She was hiding. She didn't want people to see who she was or what she looked like. What if the Caeruleus that were looking for her came close? What if her presence put Deegan in danger? She couldn't let what happened in Sheffield happen here. She just couldn't.

"I've always wanted to know. Do blondes really have more fun?" Deegan teased.

Brene laughed. "Table seven needs another round of drinks. Beatrice sees to that side," She nodded towards her right, where the server named Beatrice was taking orders from a group of rowdy customers. "Averi sees to that side," she nodded towards her left, where Averi was carrying a tray of drinks. "I'm going to drop these off at table nine and then go home to take a nice long bath." She closed her eyes and tilted her head back as she spoke the last few words.

"You know, if you keep going down this path, I might even leave this place to you when I die," Deegan said.

"Ha! Like you're ever going to die, old man." They laughed, and then Brene carried the two beers away, laid them on table nine, and waved to Deegan as she made her way to the door.

As she reached the door, a group of people walked in. Two of them were dressed in long black robes, the hoods of which settled on their shoulders. The robes were open, almost like coats, and underneath they dressed almost identically. They wore black leather pants with knee-high black combat boots, black hoodies with black leather jackets over them, and black leather gloves. Their faces were pale and lacked emotion, and both their hair was dyed a deep, raven black that seemed to absorb all light around them and create an eerie, dark air.

One of the two, a young man, flicked his long straight hair to the side, exposing the right of his head to be shaved short. The other of the two styled his hair in a Mohawk, with each side shaved clean. A third young man, his face just as pale, but a hint of kindness in his eyes, dressed in all black as well. He wore black cargo pants with many pockets down the side. His combat boots ended mid-calf, a black leather jacket over a black long-sleeve shirt, and deep red leather gloves, the color of blood. The last of the party was rather ordinary looking, compared to the other three. He was a muscularly tall man with skin the rich color of hot chocolate on a cold winter's day and a face that held warmth and benevolence. His eyes were dark and penetrating but still wonderfully gentle, and when he held Brene's gaze, it made the hairs on the back of her neck stick up.

Brene looked down, suddenly aware that she was staring, feeling a warmth inside her body that she hadn't felt in a long time.

"Excuse me," she said, still looking down, trying to move past the group and out the door.

"No," The handsome stranger spoke, his voice deep and

soothing, like stepping into a hot bath at the end of a long day. "Excuse me."

Brene looked up now. "What?" she said, confusion in her tone.

"Sorry. I just got so nervous when I saw you. I didn't know what I was saying." The stranger smiled mischievously, a glint of arrogance in his eyes now. "What's a pretty thing like you doing in a shoddy place like this?"

Men. They just have to open their mouths, and their entire appeal goes out the window. Brene thought to herself.

"Please excuse me. I have somewhere to be," Brene replied, trying not to engage for longer than necessary.

"Wherever you have to be, I think I have to be there too," the stranger leaned towards her. "Layton Murphy. It's an absolute pleasure to meet such a fine specimen as yourself. And your name is?"

"Mr. Murphy, I'm truly not interested." Brene was getting irritated. "Now, if you'll excuse me, I have somewhere to be."

"Okay. Okay," Layton held up his hands in surrender. "At least give me your number. Maybe sometime this week I'll be waiting at your somewhere to be."

"I don't think so. Good day." Brene took a step forward towards the door, but as she did, Layton quickly stepped before her, blocking her path to the door.

"Mr. Murphy," she said through gritted teeth. "If you don't step out of my way in the next three seconds—"

"You promise?" Layton winked at her.

Brene took a deep breath in, and then she dropped to the ground, stuck out her leg, and swept it before her. Her legs contacted Layton's suddenly and caused the young man to lose his balance, falling backward onto his dark, shady friends. Then Brene stood up and made her way to the exit.

CHAPTER 3

THE NEXT DAY, Brene arrived early at work and entered the bar to find Deegan mopping the floors.

"I can do that, old man," she said, pulling her sling bag over her head and placing it on the bar top.

"I got this. I need you to take a trip into town for me. I was supposed to drop off these tax filings last week, and I need some more angina potion from the apothecary." He stopped mopping, crossed one foot over the other as he stood, and leaned on the mop. "You think you can handle that without drop-kicking anyone?" he smirked.

"They guy was a jerk. He wouldn't take no for an answer," Brene rolled her eyes. "Where are the filings? In the back?"

After collecting the tax filings from the back office of the bar and writing the list of remedies that Deegan needed from the apothecary, Brene made her way into town. Riding her motorcycle slowly, since she was still unfamiliar with the area. The city center was like most others she had seen. There were tall buildings with glass windows, little parks and courtyards in-between, and traffic that could drive even the calmest soul just a little crazy.

Once she dropped off the tax filings, she walked two blocks to a large courtyard with a water fountain in the center. The water fountain was the most beautiful that Brene had ever seen. The fountain's base looked like a pirate ship in which water had pooled, the mainmast towering high into the sky. The mainsail, although sculpted from stone was so intricately mad that it looked as though it was flowing in the wind, the soft material fluttering slightly. On the masts on either side of the main, men held on with one hand and leaned outwards like a child swinging around a pole. Water sprayed outwards from their boots, falling down into the boat and, now and again, spraying onto the paving in the courtyard.

Brene looked at the fountain in awe. The only thing that could make it any more beautiful was magical creatures. But that was wishful thinking because that city was home to thousands of humans.

Finally, building up the will to look away from the entrancing fountain, she walked past it and towards a line of shops on the far side of the courtyard. Suddenly, she stopped in her tracks and felt a buzz inside her. Similar to an electric shock that heated her body suddenly from the inside out.

"That's impossible," she whispered to herself.

She turned around frantically, looking in all directions to find whatever had triggered her. Had the Caeruleus finally found her? For years, they had tried to capture her to use her powers for their own selfish gain. Sometimes she wished she wasn't born an Ipian at all. She told no one about her secret gifts.

From the beginning of time, Ipians served as the right hands to the most powerful rulers in the land. In fact, in the legend of the great jaguar shape-shifter, he too recruited an Ipian to help him gain power. Ipians were like magnets that were attracted and drawn to magic of all shapes and sizes.

The Caeruleus were looking for her to use her powers so that they could locate other powerful beings. Recruit them to their cause, causing anarchy and chaos. She couldn't let that happen.

Brene moved slowly towards the shops, looking around as she did, the buzz within her still keeping her on edge.

Wherever it's coming from, it must be close, she thought.

Just then, she heard giggling coming from an alleyway close by. She abandoned her task of going to the apothecary and followed the sound of the laughter. She moved slowly and stealthily, and as she neared the alleyway, she stood on the side and peaked in; being careful not to be noticed by those she was watching.

Brene's eyes grew wide as she watched the scene before her in the dark alleyway at the side of the courtyard. Her eyebrows moved high up her forehead, and her mouth gaped open as she tried to make sense of what she was seeing. There, in the alleyway, were two ordinary, human teenage boys doing magic. One boy held out his arms towards a pile of garbage, and the empty soda cans and fish bones swiftly levitated to eye-level. The boy clapped his hands, and the garbage fell back down suddenly.

Maybe they're Pannosus, Brene thought, a little spooked. She continued to watch them.

"Check this out," the other boy spoke now. He had yellow hair and fair skin and wore oversized clothing that was tattered and untidy. He stood tall, took a deep breath in, and then, there in the alleyway, his body rose into the air and hovered above his friend's head. "I can fly!" he said excitedly.

If they were Pannosus, they would have learned to use their powers by that age, and they would know not to practice magic in the middle of a human city. They must be human.

"Hey!" Brene shouted before she could help herself, then

she began running down the alleyway. But before she could get there, the boy with the yellow hair landed quickly on the ground, embraced his friend tightly, and then they both disappeared in a purple flash.

"How is this possible?" Brene whispered to herself, her body tingling with anxiety.

Brene ran to the apothecary, got everything on Deegan' list, and then hurried back to Eagle Rock as fast as she could. Somehow, she no longer felt safe.

CHAPTER 4

BRENE PARKED her motorcycle on the curb, directly in front of the bar's door. She ran inside and, with perhaps a little more energy than necessary, set the remedies from the apothecary on the bar top.

"Deegan!" she said earnestly. "You will never believe what I saw today," she walked around the bar. "Children. Human children."

Deegan frowned and slowly put down the glass he was wiping. He held out his hands as if attempting to calm a wild beast, a look of astonishment washing over his face.

"Brene, maybe you've been working too hard." He walked to her and gently put his hands on her shoulders, ushering her to a nearby bar stool. "Take a seat. I'll pour you a drink."

"Yes. A drink is exactly what I need. But what about the children, Deegan?" Brene folded her arms on the bar top before her and then dramatically dropped her head down into them, sighing loudly.

Deegan' forehead furrowed as he studied Brene closely. "There are human children in human cities." He was confused and sounded altogether unsure of the statement himself.

Brene slowly raised her head, a blank look on her face, and then she closed her eyes and straightened her back, taking a deep breath in. "They were doing magic, old man," she said, opening her eyes and holding his gaze, her face turning pale as she spoke.

Deegan' eyebrows scrunched together. "Brene. That's not possible," he reached out and touched her hand lovingly like a father would to his daughter, before giving her some fatherly advice. "Go home. Rest. I think you're burnt out. You've been working long shifts for the past two weeks, plus you've been sorting out the back office and all the paperwork back there. Don't think I don't see it when you don't break for lunch." Raising his eyebrow, he stared her down.

"I know what I saw," her eyes flickered with fear.

"Is everything okay? Are you in some kind of trouble?" Deegan asked, compassion and worry in his voice.

Brene wanted so badly to tell him she was an Ipian, and that what she saw was real. She didn't just see it. She felt it at the core of her being. But she didn't. Instead, she took Deegan' hand in hers, forced a smile, and nodded.

"You're right. I think I just need a bit of a break."

"Take the day off," Deegan shrugged. "I'll get one of the girls to cover your shift. Heck, take the week off. You've done wonders in this place. You deserve it."

Brene chuckled as she made her way to the door. "I think the day is just fine."

When she stepped outside, the air was pleasantly cool and fresh, and she stood for a moment just breathing it in. She looked around the street at the Pannosus all going along with their business, some happily chatting as they walked. She sighed out loudly. She knew that what she saw was no hallucination. She felt it inside her. Those humans were doing magic in a public place. Unregulated and damn foolish.

"What is going on?" she thought.

She mounted her bike, which was parked just outside the door. Still, before she could reach for her helmet that was hanging on the right handlebar, she felt a powerful hand holding her tightly, preventing her arms from moving freely. She panicked and swallowed hard, her heart beating so loudly that she heard it thumping in her head.

Before she could scream, she felt something cold and soaking wet being pressed into her face, covering her mouth and nose completely. She felt her eyes grow heavy as she inhaled the powerful scent of chloroform, trying hard not to lose consciousness. She wriggled her body with what energy she had left. Then, for a split second, she felt her body go flax before darkness engulfed her.

* * *

Brene was shivering violently, hugging her body tightly to retain heat. She opened her eyes suddenly and frantically sat up, remembering her abduction, and looked around. She was in some sort of room. The floor and walls alike seemed to each be made of a large slab of white marble. In the middle of one wall was a heavy-duty white door with large bolts along the edges and a round handle that looked to be made of clear crystal. Brene looked up to find that the ceiling was a large mirror. She studied her reflection for a moment, unable to recognize herself. Then her eyes widened, and her heartbeat quickened as she realized why the image above her looked so unfamiliar. They knew who I was, she thought, getting to her feet and pacing around the room, running her hands over the cap that she wore on her head. The cap, over which her black wig would usually sit. She had bought that wig, and the other

13 that she owned, from a shady arms dealer on her way to the big city. She thought that if she could change her appearance, then maybe, just maybe, she'd be able to live an everyday life. She had hoped with all her being that nobody could find her... but they did.

Whatever they want, I will not help them destroy this world. The thoughts running through Brene's mind grew more sinister as she paced the white room. I would rather die than help them kill millions of innocent Pannosus and humans.

The sound of big machinery moving caused Brene to stop pacing and turn to the sound source. It was the door. Brene backed up slowly to the farthest wall and stood with her back flash against it, welcoming the shock that the icy surface gifted her. She felt awake and alert.

The large door swung open sluggishly, creaking loudly as it did. The sound bounced against the white walls and creating a loud echo. The first man to walk through the door looked small and frail, his face generously sprinkled with freckles, his skin crinkled, and a little extra hanging down under his chin like the wattle of a rooster. Although few, the hairs on his head were silvery gray and smoothed back, ending in a bit of a ponytail. He wore a long dark purple robe that matched the color of his eyes perfectly and held a gold staff that was almost a head taller than him. At the top of his staff was an orb. Around the size of an average orange, the orb was made of clear glass, inside of which was the head of a jaguar. It was dark purple and shone a metallic hue, like the scales of a fish. Brene studied the man, trying to place his familiarity.

The second man was much taller than the first. He wore a countenance of kindness, and his face was long and slim; in fact, his resemblance to a locust was uncanny. He had dark brown hair that set untidily on his head and wore a pair of half-moon spectacles over his icy blue eyes that were much too dated for his youthful look. His robe was a deep blue color, like the darkest and most depths of the ocean, and looked to be made of velvet. Around his neck, he wore a golden medallion the size of a saucer. In the center of the medallion, there was an orb of clear glass, the size of a marble, and within that orb was a galaxy of stars.

The third man, who looked much older than the second but much younger than the first, wore a royal green robe with beautiful gold edging. His hair was a mixture of dark brown and gray and curled tightly, setting much like Brene's own. His skin, although mostly light, had patches of dark brown and reminded Brene of a Dalmatian puppy she had once seen. One of his eyes was a bright green and the other a bright yellow. Next to him, rubbing its body against his was a lion that stood as tall as his waist.

The frail little man with the purple robe spoke first. His voice was deep, the sense of authority in it bouncing off the white walls. "Hello, Brenley." His thin lips curved into a smile. "It's quite an honor to meet you." The man walked towards her gracefully, almost as though he were floating. "There's no need to be afraid. I am Supreme Pagzman Chahal." He bowed his head in greeting, then turned and pointed his staff toward his companions.

"This is Supreme Pagzman Armin," he pointed to the tall man with the half spectacle glasses, who smiled kindly and bowed his head. "And this is Supreme Pagzman Vano," The man with the yellow and green eyes nodded without smiling.

"You're the Supreme Pagzman of the Order," Brene said softly.

"Yes," Chahal replied. "I am the head, and these are my confidants."

That's where I know him from. I've seen him on TV. The head of the Order! Brene's mind was racing.

"I'm truly sorry for the manner of this invitation, Miss Williams, and I'm just as sorry for removing your disguise. We had to be certain that it was you," Chahal paused, then he put out his hand, and Brene's blonde wig appeared in it. He handed it to Brene, who reluctantly accepted it.

Armin and Vano walked towards where Brene and Chahal were talking and stood on either side of the head of the Order.

"We need your help, Brenley," Armin said, his voice as warm as Brene had expected.

"There hasn't been an Ipian in the Order in almost a hundred years. We need you to use your powers for good, Brenley," Vano's different colored eyes twinkled as he spoke.

Brene looked at the three men before her, unsure of what to say or do. She felt her hands grow sweaty as she clutched tightly onto her blonde wig.

"I…" she began, swallowing hard before continuing. "I think you have the wrong person."

The three Supreme Pagzmans studied her, their eyes focused and burning with purpose.

"Follow us," Chahal turned and led the way out of the white room, followed by his two confidants and Vano's giant beast. She reluctantly walked in their direction, following at a distance behind them.

Stepping out of the white room, Brene took in her surroundings with awe. She followed her captors down a passageway brightly lit with candles all along the stone walls. In between the candles, there were beautiful paintings of men and women dressed in fine clothes. As they walked on, the images turned ominous. Some showed great battles where Pannosus and other creatures alike lay on a field in pools of blood. One painting depicted the hanging of the last of the Redgarde clan, their necks evidently broken by the force of gravity opposing that of the rope. Another showed the giant shadow of a jaguar seeming to come out of a little silver box like a genie from a lamp. The shadow towered over a group of people who were on their knees, their hands raised to the skies as if in worship.

"This way, Brenley," Vano's icy voice pulled Brene back to reality, and she followed the men down a narrow flight of steps that spiraled downwards into darkness. When they reached the bottom of the staircase, Chahal breathed in deeply, and then blew out a large gust of air, causing the candles in the walls on either side of the path before them to miraculously light up, showing the area to be a dungeon of sorts.

"What is this place?" Brene asked, her voice a little shaky.

"These are the holding cells in which we keep those that do not abide by the laws before we sentence them," Chahal's voice was cold and unforgiving. He unlatched a large wrought-iron gate and entered a cell.

The party followed Chahal into the cell. On the far wall, Brene saw a familiar-looking man standing flash against the wall as if he was held against it by some sort of invisible restraints.

"Supreme Pagzman Chahal!" The man's voice was squeaky, and his face was covered in dirt and sweat. He had a dark brown beard, some areas a little crusty with dried blood, and his nose looked to be broken, dark red liquid draining from his nostrils and pooling on his upper lip. His brown eyes were filled with tears, and he was naked except for a thin piece of cloth that covered his pelvis. "Please," he pleaded as tears rolled down his cheeks, leaving a trail of clean skin amongst the dirt on his face. "That's her. That's her," his eyes widened at the sight of Brene. "I told you everything I know. Please." He was weeping now.

Brene's eyes widened in horror at the sight of the man pleading for his life.

"I swear. I sold her the wigs, and she used her powers to tell me which of the artifacts I had stolen were worth the most. That's all. I've fulfilled my end of the bargain." The man was sobbing and struggling to talk and breathe at the same time.

The three Supreme Pagzmans turned and looked at Brene, and for a long moment, nobody spoke. The only sound that could be heard was the whimpering of the man bound against the wall with some invisible, magical constraints.

Chahal sighed loudly. "Romano," he shouted toward the open cell gate.

Just then, a young man, no older than Brene herself, hurried into the room. He was wearing a black robe on top of cargo pants and a cream-colored sweater. His dark brown combat boots looked old and worn out. He looked altogether misplaced on the scene.

"Yes, Supreme Pagzman Chahal," the young man's accent was not local.

"Remove the shackles and constraints and then take him up to the infirmary. He is to be nursed back to health and then given a written warning before being sent back out."

"Yes, master," The young man bowed his head. "And what shall the warning say?"

"That if we caught him committing crimes against the code of Established Bewitchery Activity in the future," Chahal turned to face the prisoner, "he shall be sentenced to life in the mining district. An intramuscular nulling device will be inserted in an unknown location, preventing him from using any magic. Do I make myself clear, Mr. Wallace?"

The prisoner wept harder and nodded his head feverishly. "I will never go against the law again. I swear."

With that, the young man carried out his task, and Supreme Pagzman Chahal turned and walked out of the cell, followed by his confidants and Brene. They looked back for a long moment before exiting. Chahal turned to Brene and the other two and sighed loudly when the party was outside the cell.

"Tea?" he smiled.

CHAPTER 5

In Supreme Pagzman Chahal's private chamber, Brene sat by the fire. Holding her cup of tea with both her hands, she waited in a comfortable chair with a high backrest made of soft, warm, plum-colored velvet. The three Supreme Pagzmans sat before her in similar chairs, sipping their tea happily. Brene studied the men curiously, and when nobody spoke for a long while, she decided she would break the awkward silence.

"Okay. I'm an Ipian," she said, her eyes darting from one man's gaze to the other.

Chahal chuckled. "Well, we knew that."

"I swear. I have done nothing illegal. I only knew that guy because I bought a couple of wigs from him. I needed to disappear. There's this group of Caeruleus after me. They knew about my powers because I needed money, so I looked at a couple of artifacts and told them about each of their magical properties. Understand. I was alone and on the street. I had no family. There was nobody to look out for me," Brene's voice was shaky, and she could feel tears pooling in her eyes. She swallowed hard and dropped her head down, fixing her gaze on her feet.

"Did you ever use your powers on people?" Supreme Pagzman Armin asked, placing his teacup down in the saucer that he held in the other hand.

Brene closed her eyes and breathed deeply. "Once," she said, so quietly that it was almost a whisper. She pulled both her lips in then released them as she lifted her head up. "There were about four or five people in this room. The guy that I was dealing with, his name was Shein. He took me there, and he asked me what kind of magic each of them possessed. They looked scared." A look of regret washed over her face. "I told him that my powers didn't work on people, but he knew I was lying. He grabbed one of them. She was a little girl. She couldn't have been much older than fourteen, fifteen." Brene's eyes became glassy with the tears that pooled. She swallowed again. "He put his hand on her head and said that he would send shock waves through her head and explode her brain if I didn't do exactly what he said. So, I did." She looked down at her feet again and closed her eyes. "There was only one man in the group that had the power they wanted. He was an Aligist. He could understand and speak every language in the universe. So, they killed him and absorbed his power. They let the rest go."

"The Aligist, was he the first one in the group that you touched?" Chahal asked.

Brene nodded, her head still hanging low and her eyes still closed.

"Was he the only one who possessed great power?" Vano spoke next.

Brene shook her head slowly.

"Who else?" Armin's voice was warm.

"There was a woman who possessed the power of ice."

"And?" Armin urged.

"There was a man who could turn invisible at will."

"And?" Armin seemed to look for something specific.

"The little girl that Shein held. She could regenerate."

"All those abilities are only possible with the greatest power. But you knew that, didn't you?" Chahal placed his teacup on the table nearby. "You saved those Pannosus, Brenley."

"Not all of them," her voice was soft. She wiped her face with her hands and took a deep breath in. "Anyway," she continued a little louder and with a false sense of strength, "I left that night. Ran away," she nodded. "I put myself through Eagle Rock Academy, got an excellent education, and now I'm trying to make a living for myself. I don't want to be involved in that world," Brene shook her head slowly.

"We need your help, Brenley," Chahal said, compassion in his voice.

"Stop calling me that! My name is Brene. Brene." She couldn't hold the tears back any longer. She dropped her face into her hands, and her body jerked as she cried.

The three Supreme Pagzmans shared a look, and then Vano lifted his hand, flicked his wrist in a sort of twirl, allowing his fingers to dance in the air. As he lowered his hand to his lap, the giant beast that had stood by him earlier appeared behind Brene's chair. The lion moved slowly and stealthily, stopping in front of her face. He puffed out a breath of warm air that was fragranced like rich, hot chocolate. She lifted her head slowly and faced the beast, looking deep into its sapphire-colored eyes, and there she saw something quite bewildering.

In the lion's eyes that gleamed brightly like two glass orbs, she saw a shower of bright sparks from the sky, falling to earth with great speed. The Earth was soaked in incandescent light, but then the image changed. Suddenly, the Earth appeared dull, as though a sort of sickness had washed over it. She saw men and women yielding dark powers, killing those in their path. A baby girl lay lifeless on the floor, her mother's hand lying next to her head, but the rest of her body was nowhere to be seen. Then the images changed once again. She saw a man, naked, of immense stature, with his muscles defined and his body exquisite. He approached a nuptial bed to which a path of rose petals led. He reached out gently and pulled apart the curtains that dressed the bed, and there, waiting for him, was a woman whose face Brene could not see. She, too, was naked except for a beautiful silk veil across her face, as red as blood and as delicate as a flower. The man climbed onto the bed and reached out to the woman, caressing her breasts lustfully. Her back arched as she moaned at his touch. He climbed on top of her and leaned down so that his lips were against her ears, and he whispered, "The blood moon is near, my love." The man's voice echoed in Brene's head, growing louder and louder until it was a shrill scream.

Brene brought her hands to her ears and pressed them hard against her head, tucking her head down into her chest. Her head was pounding now. The pain was causing her eyes to water and a large vein in her forehead to pop out visibly. Then, once again, Brene found herself engulfed by darkness.

When she finally came to, she found herself on the comfortable chair in front of the fire in Supreme Pagzman Chahal's private quarters. The three Supreme Pagzmans were merrily talking and seemed not to notice that she had regained consciousness. Brene sat up slowly, feeling a little drowsy, and placed her hands on the armrests of the chair for balance.

"Oh, you've come back to us. Very good. You are a strong one," Supreme Pagzman Armin leaned towards her and handed her a little glass filled to the brim with a bright green liquid. "This will help with the pounding in your head," he smiled at her. Brene couldn't help but feel like although his lips were curved in a smile, his eyes did not share the same intention.

Brene reached out her hand and accepted the concoction, looking at it questionably before lifting the glass to her lips and gulping the thick, slimy liquid down. Surprisingly so, the liquid tasted like the smell of freshly cut glass and mint.

"We need your help, Brenley—" Supreme Pagzman Chahal stopped himself too late. "Brene. We need your help, Brene," he smiled kindly.

"What did you do to me?" she asked softly, "I saw—" she blinked a few times, trying to make sense of what she had seen in the beast's eyes.

"That was the prophecy," Vano explained. "Before we can tell you any more, we must know if you are willing to help us."

Brene thought for a long moment, allowing the images of what she just saw to run through her mind. She thought about her life. She hated where she lived, and although she was grateful for her job at the bar, she didn't want to spend her entire life busting tables and serving drinks. She needed to do more. She wanted to do more. And here more was, knocking on her door and asking for her help. She thinned her lips and nodded.

"Very good," Armin said excitedly, and then his tone turned serious. "Do you know the ancient tale of the Myxan?"

"Um… I know that the great shape-shifter was bound to the Myxan and his spirit lived on in there. Then it was found—"

"It wanted to be found," Armin interrupted her. Brene scrunched her eyebrows together, and Armin took her confusion as an opportunity to tell the tale himself.

"When the Myxan was created by the dark magic

possessed by the spirit of the great shape-shifter, it became an object of its own will. It urged humans and Pannosus alike to commit unspeakable and unnatural acts. When the Myxan had gained enough souls and had almost grown strong enough for the spirit of the great shape-shifter to take the form of a leopard once more, it called a meeting of its followers in a glade in the middle of the Eastern Forest."

"That's where The War of the Ancestors took place," Brene said.

"Indeed. But before the final two souls could be absorbed and the shape-shifter could take physical form once again, the Freedom Fighters of a nearby village disbanded the Redgarde cult and captured its remaining members. Executing them in the days to follow. During the Redgarde and the Freedom Fighters battle, the Myxan was dropped into a river on which layers of ice had settled. The strong current carried the box for miles and for a long time fell out of existence."

"Right. Until a few members of the Freedom Fighters found the Myxan and destroyed it. And those individuals created the council known now as the Order." She held out her hand with her palm facing the ceiling and nodded toward the three men.

The three men shared glances among them, and a moment of silence went by before Chahal spoke. "Members of the revolutionaries who destroyed the Myxan did not create the Order. It was created as a specialized task force to find the Myxan and put an end to the prophecy."

"I don't understand," Brene leaned forward. "So, when was the Myxan actually found and destroyed then? And what's this prophecy all about?"

"It wasn't," Chahal replied.

Brene's eyes flashed with confusion as she studied the three men before her. Her jaw slackened, forcing her mouth to hang open as she waited for someone to speak. When nobody spoke, she cleared her throat and prompted the conversation. "So, the Myxan is still out there?"

"Yes," Vano said, his voice still lacking emotion.

Brene got to her feet and paced the area in front of the fireplace.

"The Myxan! The darkest, most powerful magical force in the world's history is still out there somewhere." She pointed in a random direction. "So, go find it!" Her voice was becoming shrill as panic took over her body. She could feel her heart beating faster, and her stomach churned vigorously.

"That's why we need you," Vano maintained his composure. "We've put together a team to scout for the Myxan, and we need you on that team."

Brene continued to pace frantically. "And what about this prophecy?"

"Well, when the leader of the Redgarde clan was being executed, right before, he spoke of a prophecy," Armin explained. "The words have been passed down through the generations, so the prophecy is well known among us, but it's not complete. We only know the first part." Armin leaned forward now, "The prophecy has begun to reign true, Brene. We need to find the Myxan before it's too late."

"What do you mean reign true?" Brene stopped her pacing and faced the Supreme Pagzman Armin. He reached inside his robe and pulled out a piece of discolored cloth. He handed it to Brene, who read the words carefully.

The concord inscribed will bring by false peace
As cozenage and truth engulfs all you know
The hate and the darkness will only increase
The heat of the great orb melting the snow
Dark magic shall burgeon and fill up the air
And the Cursed One will rise—

"I don't understand," Brene read over the words again.

"The concord, it's the Covenant of Assimilation, Integration, and Association. Its aim is to ultimately address the human-Pannosus disparity. I fear the peace that it has brought will be short-lived," Chahal said.

"That proves nothing, Supreme Pagzman Chahal," Brene tried to sound respectful.

"The heat of the great orb melting the snow. It's the recent solar flares. There have been many places where the snow has all melted. And the dark magic that the prophecy speaks of... There have been sightings of humans possessing magical abilities. It's unnatural."

Brene thought back to the boys in the alleyway. She knew in her gut that the Supreme Pagzman was right. The prophecy was unraveling.

"Alright," Brene said. "Where do we begin?"

CHAPTER 6

BRENE DIDN'T KNOW what to expect as she followed the three Supreme Pagzmans away from the warmth of the fire and back into the eerie passageway that was illuminated by candles against the rock walls. This time, instead of descending, they took a staircase that took them upwards. Although the spiral stairs and walkway were exceptionally narrow, and Brene felt a little claustrophobic, she pushed her fears away from her mind and focused on the mission at hand.

Supreme Pagzman Chahal spoke when they reached a landing as he led the way down a large hallway adorned with framed paintings on the rock walls on either side. The floor was covered in a dark red Persian runner that seemed to run the length of the passage. Against the walls, in between large murals of people and scenery, there were sculptures as large as Brene herself, each of which looked to be sculpted from one massive piece of marble. There was one of a naked man that posed as though he was sitting and thinking hard. Another was a beautiful woman whose hands were outstretched and in her hands. There were pedestals along the walls on which objects sat, some covered in clear glass boxes, and some exposed to the elements around.

"We have put together a team of Pannosus," Chahal began. "They have been tasked with finding the Myxan and bringing it back to us. Three of the individuals are… well… they're Verdigris," he lowered his voice as he spoke the last few words, as though the fact embarrassed him.

Brene's eyebrows raised, "Verdigris?" she blinked a few times. "You've formed a team with Pannosus who practice dark magic." Brene was regretting volunteering her services at all.

"They simply believe that all magic should be practiced, and none prohibited," Chahal said, sounding like he was trying to convince himself more than Brene.

"They're radical," Brene said softly, allowing her focus to be drawn in by the beautiful displays as she walked down the hallway.

"Yes, well, we required skill and power for such a mission," Chahal stopped outside two large wooden doors that had the symbol of a jaguar's head engraved in the center, half of the face setting on each door. He pushed the doors open, splitting the head of the engraved jaguar, and led the way into the room.

The first thing that welcomed Brene as she stepped into the room was the warmth from the fire burning. The warm air on her skin comforted her greatly and made her feel at ease. As she stepped into the room, she looked around curiously, inhaling the scene before her, her eyes gleaming excitedly. She and three Supreme Pagzmans seemed to stand on a platform that spanned the edges of the entire room. A little way before her, three steps led down into a sunken study of sorts. She walked down the steps slowly, her head tilted up all the while as she took in the surrounding room.

The room was enormous, the ceiling so high that she had

to squint to locate the wooden rafters that supported the roof above. To her left, three great bay windows spanned from the ground to the ceiling and made the room appear to be made of glass. The window frames were made of dark wood and arched towards the top. Almost as though she were in a room in an ancient castle. The windows were dressed with heavy-looking black velvet curtains that were drawn to the sides. Brene looked through the window at the sky that was darkening outside. It was later in the day than she had thought.

On the wall directly opposite the door, a fireplace emitted tremendous heat, above which a mural that took up almost was the entire wall itself. The mural depicted a scene from the stories of The War of the Ancestors. A young man was reaching for the Myxan that sat on the stone pedestal in the middle of the glade as those around him fought.

The wall to the right was covered from floor to ceiling in dark brown bookshelves that seemed to overflow with books and manuscripts. Two ladders on opposite sides of the wall leaned against the shelves, the bases attached to a track that ran the room's width next to the shelves. Some comprehensive books were placed piled in front of the shelves, and pieces of parchment were scattered around on the floor. The room was furnished exquisitely, with the center being occupied by a set of couches and a round, dark brown coffee table that sat on top of a dark green Persian rug. The floors were made of the same dark wood as the window frames. The room was so large that it was divided into different areas. Closest to the bookshelves on the wall, there was a magnificent round table made of a glossy type of wood that was red in hue. On the table, various books and parchments were laid out untidily. Closest to the window, there were displays like those she had seen in the hallway as they walked, just moments ago, and a large stone pedestal around which four people were huddling, looking down at a piece of parchment that was laid out.

Chahal cleared his throat, and the group slowly lifted their heads towards Brene and the three Supreme Pagzmans.

Brene scrunched her eyebrows and tilted her head as she looked at the group huddled around the pedestal. Then her eyes widened, and her mouth gaped open as she realized why they seemed so familiar.

"You," she spat, surprise in her voice.

Before her stood the handsome young man with whom she had an unenjoyably encounter at Deegan' bar. A meeting ended in her happily leaving the bar. The handsome stranger was lying on the floor with his ego terribly bruised. He smirked mischievously and strolled towards her, the other three following suit. He was dressed almost the same as the first time they had met: dark brown cargo pants, a navy-blue button-down shirt, mid-calf combat boots, and a dark brown leather jacket. Only now he had the home-court advantage.

He held out his hand cordially. "I think we got off on the wrong foot last time." He blinked innocently, his eyes twinkling as he gave Brene a half-smile, half-smirk.

Brene reluctantly took his hand, surprised at the warmth that it held, and narrowed her eyes at the handsome man. She forced a thin smile and nodded. "Maybe I was a little too quick to judge."

"You know each other?" Supreme Pagzman Chahal studied the two curiously, his eyebrows rose.

"We've met before," the man reassured him.

"Very good. I will leave you to get properly acquainted. And may I just say," he paused, "Brenley is a lovely name. One should never forsake the name of one's ancestor."

Brene snorted, "I appreciate that, but they named me after my mother's favorite chocolate. Brenley Kisses."

A look of concern washed over the Supreme Pagzman's

face before he bowed his head to Brene and then turned on his heels and led his two confidants out of the room, closing the doors behind them. The inside of the door had the exact engraving as the outside: an intricate image of a jaguar's head split equally between the two doors.

Brene stood for a moment, feeling awkward in the new company. The other three men in the room were dressed the same as the night when she met them. But for very slight differences that perhaps she didn't entirely observe in their initial meeting. The man with the deep red leather gloves was the first to step forward and offer his hand to her. Smiling kindly, his eyes the color of the inside of a grapefruit that was ready to eat.

"Joel Pardo," he nodded as Brene took his hand. A wave of red light pulsated through his pale skin at Brene's touch, and he stepped back, an impressed look on his face. "An Ipian, ay?" His thick cockney accent mixed with the enthusiasm in his voice made Brene chuckle, and she nodded slowly.

"How did you know?" she asked curiously, narrowing her eyes at Joel and holding his gaze.

"I'm not a natural Ipian, but I learned how to harness magnetic powers. It's nothing fancy. I can just tell what someone's strengths are by drawing a little of their power. So little that you wouldn't even notice that I did." He smiled.

Brene couldn't help but feel like she had misjudged the Verdigris based on preconceived notions. Joel Pardo seemed kind and warm, and she was growing comfortable in his company. His short, jet-black hair was shaved on the sides. Set in a ponytail on the top of his head, black strands like shards of glass shot up and out like a fountain. To Brene's liking, he kind of resembled a unicorn.

The other two men in dark clothing edged closer and stuck out their hands one by one.

"Moria Fox," the one with a Mohawk said without smiling. Brene tried to contain her surprise at the high pitch of the individual's voice. It was a woman. Now that Brene saw her face up close, she looked quite beautiful. With delicate features, her lovely deep blue eyes, like the color of the sea during the violent tempests of night.

Brene took her gloved hand. Moria held her hand longer than necessary and looked deep into her eyes, never blinking or allowing any emotion to flow into her countenance. When she finally released her hand, she nodded in approval at the others in the room.

"Ramdeo Baksh," the man with the half-shaved head smiled. "Don't mind Moria. She's a creature of very few words. She's also not trusting of people, but you got the nod of approval."

Brene smiled back, releasing a breath that she wasn't aware she was holding, feeling relieved and a little lighter.

Then, the handsome man she had first laid eyes on jumped in front of Brene and held his hands up in surrender. "Layton Murphy. But I'm sure you knew that." He smirked, and Brene rolled her eyes, struggling to conceal her smile.

"You can call me Brene," she nodded and held each man's gaze for a few moments before spinning on her heels and looking up at the ceiling. "This place is amazing," her voice was full of awe and wonder, and the men watched her closely as she looked around like a child experiencing the world for the very first time.

After a few moments, Layton placed his hands on her shoulders.

"Yes, that's all very nice, but we have a task to do."

He ushered her towards the stone pedestal around which they were all huddled when she had entered, but she turned her head and gave him a look as to say, if you touch me again, I will kill you. Layton retracted his hands from her shoulders and held them up in surrender, once again smirking, all the while mischievously.

"I like a challenge," he said, holding her gaze.

Brene felt herself enthralled by Layton's dark, penetrating eyes before forcing herself to look away, shaking off the goosebumps that his presence caused on her skin.

Moria, Ramdeo, and Joel lead the way to the pedestal, and each placed their hands on the creased parchment that was laid out, flattening it so that they could read the words.

"How much do you know?" Moria asked. Her pale face still devoid of emotion.

"Only that the Myxan was never destroyed and is somewhere out there. And we need to locate it and bring it back to the Order," Brene replied.

Moria nodded. "So, not much at all."

Brene opened her mouth to speak, but before she could, Ramdeo took center stage.

"No matter," he smiled. "We'll fill you in."

He flipped the piece of parchment so that the writing could be read from where Brene stood and pointed at a couple lines of words in the topmost corner. "This is what the head of the Redgarde clan prophesied right before his execution."

The words were the same as those she had heard earlier in the Supreme Pagzman's private chambers. Brene nodded knowingly.

"From what we know," Ramdeo continued, "the solar flares originate from the great planet of Rimia. It's a fire planet in our galaxy. It's further away than we initially calculated. Still, pieces of its crust were broken off during a meteor shower on the planet, and those pieces made their way into our atmosphere," he paused and waited for Brene to nod before continuing. "Rimia is a planet that's...." Ramdeo looked up, squinting his eyes, looking for the right word.

"Different from most. Here on Earth, and in most other planets that sustain life, the magic is contained in the beings that live on the planet. The magic of Rimia is housed in its core."

Brene scrunched her eyebrows. "So, the pieces of the core that fell to the Earth held magic?"

Ramdeo nodded. "And power."

"But what does that have to do with the solar flares?" Brene asked.

"A couple of pieces of the Rimia's core were sucked in by a vacuum surrounding the sun, and since it was used to high temperatures, it didn't disintegrate before reaching the sun's surface. That's what caused the first solar flare. That was before any of the core had even entered the Earth's atmosphere yet."

Brene frowned. "Okay, but what does any of that have to do with the Myxan?"

"The first solar flare happened naturally. It was the will of the universe," Joel said. "But that flare caused a surge of energy that pulsated throughout our entire galaxy. Earth included. And that energy is what awakened the Myxan after all this time."

"And after that," Moria spoke, "it seems like the Myxan used whatever power it had left to facilitate the meteor shower on Rimia. Allowing pieces of the planet's core to break away and land on the sun's surface, which caused the twelve solar flares that we've accounted for."

"Around the fifth solar flare is when we had a meteor shower in the East," Layton said. "Pieces of Rimia's core fell into the enchanted forest that sits along the Mendi Mountains. The power and magic from the Rimia's core seem to be flowing around the Earth erratically, causing humans to develop magical abilities and unleashing havoc among the creatures of the dark. Last week we hunted a were-creature that could transform into numerous different animals. An alligator, a giant eagle—"

"A fucking bear." Joel pulled the collar of his sweater down to show a healing wound that looked to be made by sharp claws. There were four deep lashes across his collarbone and down across his chest.

"Each solar flare made the Myxan progressively more powerful, and each meteor shower gave the Earth more power, causing more humans to transform into 'synthetic Pannosus.'" Layton used air quotes as he spoke the last few words. "But as soon as the humans use their newfound powers, it sort of slowly powers up the Myxan. Then when the humans go crazy and use their powers full force, their souls become bound to the Myxan and can be used as a constant energy supply, draining the humans the more magic they use. Eventually, they end up being like zombies. Drained of all their energy. Slaves to the Myxan and its magic."

"And now, you're filled in," Ramdeo smiled and shrugged.

"Wait, so the more humans use their powers, the more powerful the Myxan gets, eventually draining the humans and taking their souls. Then what? What's the endgame? What's the big climax?" Brene was trying hard to place all the facts together cohesively.

"The great shape-shifter retakes physical form and destroys the world," Layton said matter-of-factly.

"Okay. I think I'm on par now. What's the plan?" Brene's eyes darted from one man's gaze to the next.

Moria placed her index finger on the part of the parchment that looked like a map. "We go here."

CHAPTER 7

On a green hill in the East, just a little way away from the enchanted forest that climbed the initial uphill of the Mendi Mountains, there was a bright yellow flash. Then, a ball of light appeared floating in the air, slowly sinking towards the ground of lush green grass. The ball of light grew larger until it burst, and a group of four individuals appeared on the grass, standing tall and taking in their surroundings. A fifth individual appeared on all fours.

Brene's eyes were watering, and her stomach was churning as she allowed her fingers to grip tightly onto the grass, digging them deep into the ground. Then, without warning, she hurled the contents of her stomach out before wobbling into a standing position. She turned to face the others, wiping her mouth with the back of her hand and re-positioning the knapsack on her back.

"It happens to the best of us," Ramdeo offered before turning his attention back to his surroundings.

Moria reached into her cloak and pulled out a little bright green potion bottle. She offered it to Brene. "The first time I traveled through a long-distance portal, I passed out completely. Here, this will make you feel better."

Brene was grateful for Moria's compassion and accepted the potion bottle, and then she gulped down its contents. She thanked Moria, then returned the empty potion bottle and took in her surroundings.

"Where exactly are we?" Brene asked.

"That's the enchanted forest." Joel pointed down the hill at the collection of tall, ominous-looking trees that seemed to go on forever in all directions. "And those are the Mendi Mountains," he pointed above the forest at a range of mountains in the distance made of about a dozen peaks, some capped in snow and some dry and brown.

"This is where the first burst of energy came from. We should scout the area. There might be some sort of residual magic that we could pick up on." Ramdeo began walking down the steep hill, and the others followed.

As they walked down the hill and towards the enchanted forest, mountains and trees alike seemed to move further away. The closer they thought they were getting, the further away their destination seemed.

"I can carry that for you, you know," Layton nodded towards Brene's knapsack. "A pretty thing like you shouldn't be carrying an ugly thing like that," he smirked.

Brene stopped walking and re-adjusted her knapsack once again, and then she turned to Layton and held his gaze for a long time, narrowing her eyes, before speaking. "I can handle myself, Layton. Or don't you remember?"

She walked around him and continued to follow the rest of the group. She saw a smirk flash across Moria's face as she passed her, and Brene was feeling very comfortable in the girl's company. Maybe, just maybe, she had found a friend in Moria. Brene couldn't remember the last time she had a friend or someone to talk to. She had been running for so long and had gotten so used to a life of isolation. Even at school, she would keep to herself and focus on her studies rather than social events and activities.

After walking for about two hours, they had reached a massive canyon that stood in their way. They stood at the bottom of the canyon; the pathway leading into the rocky terrain appearing ominous.

Joel, who was leading the group, reached the inside of his leather jacket and pulled out a piece of parchment that was severely discolored and tattered in certain areas. The parchment was folded closed and sealed with the emblem of a jaguar's head, its eyes focused and unforgiving.

"Ramdeo," Joel said, as he squatted down and laid the piece of parchment on the ground, "open it."

Ramdeo closed his eyes and breathed in deeply, and then he made a fist with his right hand and blew into it hard. Brene's eyes widened with wonder as she watched fire escape the young man's breath, allowing his fist to glow from the inside out. Then Ramdeo crouched down and held his hand above the map, the heat melting the jaguar seal. As the seal heated, the jaguar's head came to life and roared loudly. Then it shook its head, closed its eyes, and bowed before the wax seal disintegrated into the air. Joel opened the parchment and flattened it out on the ground as the rest of the group hovered around him. It was a map.

"We must be here," he pointed on the map. "This is a canyon." He moved his finger along the map, "and this is the enchanted forest."

"I don't like it," Layton said, studying the map closely. "There's something not right. I say we go around."

"We'd lose at least a whole day, Layton," Joel looked up at him. "If we go through here," he ran his finger along with the map, "then we could make it to the mountain in the next three days."

"What's that?" Layton pointed to an almost invisible inscription at the base of the canyon on the map.

Joel squinted his eyes and moved his head closer to read the inscribed words.

"It's some kind of inscription," he looked up at Moria. "It's in some other tongue."

Moria held her hands in front of her, and Joel gently laid the map in her outstretched hands. Moria closed deep blue eyes, and when she opened them, they appeared a light gray. She cast her gaze on the inscription on the map.

…The pure shall come into their power

And spill their own blood on the hour…

After reading the inscription out loud, she closed her eyes once again, and when she opened them, they were the deep blue color of the sea.

"The inscription isn't complete. Looks like the entire map isn't complete." She handed the map back to Joel. "Maybe Layton's right. We should go around." Then she turned to Layton. "Are you getting anything?"

"Just a bit of a buzz, really. Nothing too powerful," Layton looked up at the rocky sides of the canyon.

"You need some juice?" Moria offered him her hand as if they had just met and were about to shake them, but Layton shook his head, a serious look on his face, and paced.

All the while, Brene watched the group closely, her gaze darting from one member to another. Then, suddenly, all the pieces came together in her mind, and she gasped loudly.

"You're an Ipian!" She pointed at Layton, who stopped his pacing and faced her.

Brene wondered why they needed her if they already had an Ipian on the team.

"Yeah, so?" He shrugged, and then continued his pacing. His mind was obviously preoccupied.

Brene watched him pace and for a long moment before speaking again. There were so many thoughts rushing through her mind. She was excited that she had finally found another like herself. But she was angry that he hadn't told her sooner. She felt hopeful that there was someone here to teach her how to use her powers. But she feared the power she possessed.

"So, now what?" Brene asked, looking around at the group.

"I say we go through the canyon," Joel was the first to say. "It will save a lot of time."

"What about the inscription?" Moria asked. "We don't know what the rest of it says. Maybe we should go around."

"We're in the East, Moria," Ramdeo said. "There's bound to be something else that lay in our path that's just as enchanted as this place." He threw his hand in the gorge's direction. "So, I say we go through it. At least it's on the map that the Order gave us, so we know that they've been here and charted the place. Plus, what does pure even mean? These maps were drawn centuries ago. I'm sure it means nothing."

After a few more moments of discussion, the group took the path through the canyon and cut out a day in their journey. There were still a few hours of daylight left, so they doubled their speed as they made their way through the rocky path. As they walked, Joel still leading the way, Brene slowed down her pace to fall far enough behind to be walking next to Layton, who was anchoring the group. She couldn't help but feel that he was worried and on edge.

"You okay?" Brene asked him.

"Yeah, fine," His eyes were fixed upwards, darting from one rocky structure to another.

"How come I felt nothing?" she asked curiously.

"I've been using my powers since I was a child. I learned how to use them and control them. You probably just haven't used them enough yet. Plus, for specialized sects, like Ipians or Aligists," he nodded in Moria's direction, "I don't know why, but when you lose your virginity, it's like all the power within you is released for your control."

"What do you mean?" Brene asked.

"Well, according to the lore, a virgin is untouched and pure. And losing one's virginity is a sacred right into power. That's why all the prophecies state that consummating a marriage with a virgin will bring you and the virgin great power. Now, I'm not saying that you can't be powerful if you're a virgin. I've seen a couple of mighty powerful ones," Layton chuckled, and Brene rolled her eyes. "But once an individual from a specialized sect loses their virginity, they become more powerful than they ever imagined."

Layton looked at Brene. "Didn't you feel the surge of power when you... you know?"

Brene felt her face turn a bright shade of pink, the heat in her cheeks almost unbearable. She tried to walk a little faster so that Layton would not see, but he kept up with her, then leaned close to her face and gasped loudly.

"Sweet mother of the dragon, you're a virgin!" He laughed. "No way!"

Brene tried to walk faster, her face burning up all the while.

"So, what?" she spat.

"So, nothing," Layton stopped laughing, and his voice took a tone of compassion. "So, why'd you wait so long?"

"I don't know," Brene spoke softly, still looking down as they walked.

"You know, the first time isn't always enjoyable. But I could make it enjoyable if you let me."

Brene looked up at Layton and saw a smug look on his face. "You know, I thought we could have a real conversation, but clearly, I was wrong. I wouldn't sleep with you if you were the last person on the face of the Earth, Layton Murphy." Then she sped up and made her way towards Moria, who was quite a distance away.

CHAPTER 8

As the sky darkened and the sun tucked itself away behind them, the group slowed down their pace.

"It'll be completely dark soon. Maybe we should set up camp here," Ramdeo offered.

"I don't like it," Ishaan replied. "The place is too open. Let's move a little further on and try to find some rock coverage."

As they walked on, Brene heard a voice as soft as silk.

Brenley.

Brene jumped with fright and looked around frantically.

"Did you guys hear that?" she asked, but the rest of the group had moved along. She was now at the back, too far away to be heard by the others.

Brenley.

The voice was that of a woman, and the more Brene looked around in the fading light of the day, the more she felt panicked.

"Who's there?" she asked, spinning around on her heels.

I am not there. I am here. The voice seemed close and echoed in

*her head, causing her temples to throb. She instinctively raised her
hands and held her head in them. I am within you.*

"Within me?" she whispered. "You're in my head?"

I am.

Brene released the hold on her head.

"What do you want?" she whispered.

*I want nothing that you do not want, Brenley. We want the
same thing. To be happy and free. Freedom comes with only one
thing. Death.*

Brene listened attentively to the voice in her head, all the
while looking up at the sky in between the large rock
surfaces surrounding her.

*You have lived a hard life, sweet Brenley. So hard and so unfor-
giving. Yet, you have grown strong.*

The voice was mesmerizing, and its words rang so true
that Brene couldn't help but believe them.

*You have risen above the odds and made your own way. But it's
tiring. I see that.*

Tears pooled in Brene's eyes now.

"It is tiring," she whispered.

You must rest, sweet girl. You deserve to rest.

"I deserve rest," Brene allowed the tears to fall down her
cheeks.

You are so alone, sweet girl. You have always been so alone.

Brene whimpered as she cried.

End your suffering, child. Rest. Brene nodded violently. She
dropped her knapsack onto the floor and wiped her face
with the back of her hands. Then she reached into her knapsack and felt around for her knife.

"I have earned this," she whispered to herself. "I have
earned this peace. I will no longer suffer. I will no longer run.
I deserve peace. I will no longer suffer."

Brene felt a hand on her shoulder and instinctively

grabbed it, pulling a heavy body forward to the ground before her.

"It's me. It's me," Layton held his hands out in surrender. "Are you alright? You fell behind. I came back to get you. The rest of the group is setting up camp just behind those rock formations over there." He got up slowly and pointed to the formations.

Brene blinked at him and shuddered as she breathed in and out.

"Brene." There was concern in Layton's voice. "You're shaking." He took off his jacket and placed it over Brene's shoulders, exposing his lean and muscular body. Then he grabbed Brene's knapsack and ushered her towards the camp.

All the while, Brene was silent. She felt entranced by the voice in her head only moments earlier, and she felt bitterness towards Layton. He had prevented her from attaining the peace that she so rightfully deserved. She yearned for the voice to come back. To tell her what she needed to do.

"I'm sorry about earlier," Layton said as they walked. "I was a jerk."

Brene continued to walk, hearing Layton's words, but not allowing them to settle in her mind. She was focused on the task at hand. She had to end her own suffering. Nobody else would do it for her. She deserved to be at peace after all that running away. After all the bad things she had done. The things she was forced to do. She deserved to be happy. It wasn't her fault. None of it was her fault.

"Come on, Brene. Say something. I mean it, truly. I'm sorry. Can we start over?" Layton turned to face her. "My gosh, Brene." He dropped the knapsack to the ground and rushed to her. "You don't look too good."

Brene's face was losing color, and her lips were cracking

and turning an eerie shade of blue. Her eyes were sinking into their sockets, making her appear ill and worn out.

"I feel fine." There was a blank look in her eyes as she spoke.

She walked past Layton and continued towards the rock formation, stepping over the knapsack on the floor and looking straight ahead. Her hands were by her sides as she walked, attempting to hold on to the jacket that Layton had placed on her shoulders. As she walked, the Jacket slipped off, falling to the ground, but she continued on as if she did not notice, like a sleepwalker with little care for the world around her.

Layton watched her as she walked, keeping his distance, carrying the knapsack and jacket.

As Brene turned the corner around a few humongous rock features, Moria and Ishaan came into sight.

"Thank goodness," Ishaan said. "We thought something had happened to you."

Brene did not say a word. She sat down next to the fire that was burning brightly and hugged her knees. Brene stared into the fire, but she saw Moria and Layton share a concerned look in the corner of her eyes.

"There's nothing to worry about. I'm fine. Just a little tired," Brene said in a monotone and emotionless voice. "May I have my knapsack, Layton?" she held out her hand without moving her gaze from the flames.

Layton reluctantly hooked one strap of the knapsack onto Brene's arm and took a seat next to her as Brene rummaged through her things. Suddenly, Brene stood up and threw the bag at Layton, fire in her eyes. Layton dodged the bag just in time and swiftly stood, taking a step back.

"What the fuck?"

"Where is it?" Brene asked.

"I don't know what you're talking about," Layton said,

scrunching his eyebrows together, his dark eyes holding her gaze.

"My knife. You took it." Brene was squeezing her hands into fists, her heart beating hard in her chest. "Give it to me."

"Brene, why would I take your knife? I have my own." Layton was standing his ground, a serious countenance washing over him.

Moria and Ishaan stood and shifted their eyes from Layton to Brene, confused looks on their faces.

Just then, Ramdeo appeared, holding a large hare by the skin on its neck. "Look what I found." He held up his prey proudly. "Ah, man! I forgot how thrilling it was to hunt."

"Please," Moria rolled her eyes. "I bet you used a luring spell." She took the hare in her hands. "I'll prepare it." She stood, studying Brene hard for a long moment before walking away from the campsite.

The tension around the fire was still very much present, and Brene never lifted her gaze from Layton's.

"What did I miss?" Ramdeo asked slowly, making eye contact with Ishaan. He widened his eyes and shrugged before throwing a couple more pieces of wood into the fire.

Brene dropped her gaze to the ground and sat back down, and for the rest of the night, she was silent.

After preparing the hare by draining all its blood, removing its skin and internal organs, and dividing the carcass into pieces, Moria levitated the game over the fire, allowing it to cook. Once everyone had eaten, Ishaan removed his jacket and reached for a little white box into the inside pocket. It was as small as those in which engagement rings were usually packaged, with intricate gold inscriptions and one large ruby on the lid. Ishaan placed the box on the ground a small distance away from the fire and removed the lid. Then, he put the lid in the palm of his left hand and gently stroked the ruby with his right index finger. The box on the floor sunk into the ground, and five sleeping bags appeared, as well as a few camping supplies and blankets.

"You should get some rest," Moria said to Brene. "You don't look too good."

With that, Brene rose from her seat like a zombie and walked to the sleeping bag furthest away from the campfire. She slid into the bag and closed her eyes, falling into a deep sleep almost immediately.

* * *

"WHAT THE FUCK is wrong with her?" Moria turned to Layton and spoke in hushed tones.

"I don't know. I think it's the magic in this place. It's having some effect on her," Layton dropped his head into his hands. "When I found her, she was going through her bag, tears running down her face, muttering I deserve peace. I will no longer suffer. And the look in her eyes, Moria," Layton shook his head. "She was furious."

"Did you take her knife?" Moria asked.

Layton reached into his boot and pulled out a small knife with a wooden grip. He handed the knife to Moria, who accepted it and twirled it around in her hands.

"Why'd you take it?" Ramdeo asked.

"I don't know. I just felt like I had to. I felt like if I didn't, something bad would happen." Layton dropped his head back and sighed loudly, and then he faced his friends again.

"Have you spoken to her about being an Ipian?" Ishaan placed a brotherly hand on his shoulder.

"Not yet. I'm scared it'll be too much for her to handle. Plus, I wouldn't know where to begin," Layton sighed again.

"What if we don't pick up any residual magic in the area?" Moria asked. "Then what?"

"Moria is right," Ramdeo said softly. "The three Supreme

Pagzmans might like us and believe that we're not bad people, but we're Verdigris after all. How long until the rest of the Order puts out a warrant for our arrest? Chahal won't be able to protect us forever."

"What are you saying?" Ishaan's eyes had grown wide. "We wanted to make a difference, and we are even though our beliefs differ from the Order's. We've proven that you don't need to be a law-abiding Pannosus to be good. And more than that, you're not bad if you believe something different to the majority."

"Ishaan," Moria placed a hand on his knee. "Someday, we're no longer going to be of use to the Supreme Pagzmans of the Order. You think they're going to keep us on the payroll and treat us with dignity?" She shook her head.

No one spoke for a long while as they all looked deep into the fire burning before them and thought hard about their choices.

"Maybe we should run," Ramdeo said in almost a whisper. "We can go somewhere tropical and open up a little beach café." He smiled longingly.

"I can whip up one mean moonshine, but you all knew that," Moria chuckled, and the group chuckled at the thought of the last time they had chugged down Moria's moonshine. They had all four of them, awoke naked in the middle of a salamander's cave, covered in honey with swords bound to each of their hands. They had quite an enjoyable experience fighting that salamander together, the blood of which unbound the swords.

"You know, I kept a bit of salamander blood," Moria said, poking the fire with a stick. "Just in case."

"I wish I had thought of that." Ramdeo rested his head in his hand. "It would have made getting out of that love bind with Leticia much easier."

They all laughed again and then fell into another moment of quiet reflection, the only sound the crackling of the fire.

"You know," Layton was the first to break the quiet. "You don't have to stay. None of you."

Ishaan grunted. "Yeah, right. Then who's going to save your butt when the time comes?"

Layton smiled. "I want you all to know, I could never have asked for a better family," he held each of their gazes.

"So, what do you think? The Ipian girl? Could she be the other half of your set?" Moria nodded in the direction in which Brene was fast asleep.

"I hope so, Moria. I truly hope so."

CHAPTER 9

YOU DESERVE TO BE FREE, child. You deserve to feel peace. You have run for too long, far too long. End your suffering. End your pain. Be free. Be happy.

Brene's eyes opened as she sat up in her sleeping bag. She turned her head to the side to see Moria in the bag closest to her. Layton and Ramdeo slept peacefully a little further away. Ishaan was nowhere to be seen, leading Brene to believe that he was on watch duty and must have taken a stroll around the area.

In the bag, child. The voice in Brene's head was now louder than ever, and the silkiness had turned into a sort of slither. She saw a black pouch to the side of Moria's sleeping bag, about the size of a pillow, which she knew contained knives and blades that Moria had warned her once before not to touch.

Brene rose stealthily from her sleeping bag and made her way towards the pouch. Then she crouched down and reached for the leather straps that bound it shut, but the leather would not budge.

"Magic," Brene whispered.

You, too, are magic, sweet child. Harness your energy so that you may be free. The suffering will end. The pain will end.

Brene closed her eyes and breathed deeply in, and then she placed both her hands on the tied leather knot and focused her energy. Her hands glowed. Warmth emanated from within her, as light flowed from her hands like ribbons dancing in the air and threading itself through the leather knot that kept Moria's black pouch sealed. Brene opened her eyes and watched as the knot untied itself before her, and the pouch opened out, displaying blades and knives that shone beneath the glow of her hands. She reached down and picked up a dagger with a brown-yellow grip and copper pummel that contained intricate circular patterns.

What beautiful details. The voice in her head echoed as she caressed the pummel with her fingers. What a privilege to have your suffering ended by such a stunning piece of metal.

Brene smiled, mesmerized by the blade as she turned it in her hands. End it, sweet child, the voice urged her on, sounding jovial and excited. End it now.

Brene held the grip in her right hand and placed the steel edge of the dagger on the inside of her left wrist. She breathed heavily as she expected the sting of the steel on her flesh.

Freedom is within reach. Cut, sweet child. Your suffering will end.

Brene dug the silver blade into her flesh, the pain-causing her heart to beat faster, pounding loudly in her chest.

"What the fuck!" Moria violently pushed her sleeping bag away and stood, grabbed the dagger with one of her hands and Brene's wrist with the other.

She looked down at the blood seeping out of the wound that Brene created. Then, she took a deep breath in and blew onto the wound, healing it completely, the blood around drying on the skin. Then Moria flung Brene's wrist away and crouched down to clean her dagger.

"Don't fucking touch my blades. Did you hear me?" Moria shouted as she tended to her dagger.

She has denied you! The voice in Brene's head had grown angry. She doesn't want you to be free. She wants you to suffer. No matter. She can be of use. Let her end it for you. It will be her gift of apology.

"Or what?" Brene challenged Moria.

Moria stood slowly and took a step towards Brene. "Or I'll kill you, Ipian."

"I bet you've killed your fair share, anyway. I'm sure killing me would be no big deal to a murderer like you," Brene chuckled, an eerie tone in her voice.

Moria's eyes widened with fury, and she pressed her lips together. "You don't know what you're talking about, Ipian."

"Oh? You're all Verdigris, aren't you?" Brene motioned to the rest of the group. "Radical and unpredictable. Don't you believe that all magic should be practicable? I bet you've done your fair share of blood sacrifices." Brene's eyebrows raised and nodded her head.

"You know nothing about us," Moria spat, the fury growing within her.

"Well then, enlighten me," Brene giggled. "Get it? En-light-en me. But you can't because you're so dark." Brene held her stomach and laughed. "But seriously, why don't you two act like you're a couple? Are you going through some-thing? Is he fucking somebody else?"

Moria had finally reached her breaking point. She leaped forward and pushed Brene to the ground, and then she got on top of her and punched her face.

"Shut the fuck up!" Moria shouted, holding her fist in the air.

"Moria!" Ramdeo shouted, hurriedly getting out of his sleeping bag. The entire group was up now.

Brene continued to laugh, spitting blood out of her mouth as she did.

"I hear that some Verdigris even sacrifice their own children. Is that true, Moria? You look like you're pretty old now. Did you have any kids? Or did you eat their hearts to be able to talk to animals?"

Moria swallowed hard, tears pooling in her eyes as she clenched her jaw.

"Did you and Ramdeo ever try again after you killed the first two? You must get some real bonus powers when you sacrifice twin babies, right?"

Moria dropped her fist hard, hitting Brene's face once again, and again, and again. Breathing heavily until Ramdeo grabbed her from behind and pulled her off Brene's barely conscious body.

Brene heard a deep, warm voice engulfing her whole. A white light coming down from the heavens surrounded her.

"I'm free," she whispered, gurgling through the blood that was pooling in her mouth. She blinked slowly, with each blink, her eyelids growing heavier until everything around her turned dark.

* * *

"Brene!" Layton cupped the back of Brene's neck and lifted her head.

Ramdeo was holding Moria as she whimpered in his arms.

"She's still breathing," Layton said as he laid two of his fingers on Brene's neck, just underneath her jawbone. "What happened? Where's Ishaan?" Layton's voice then panic-stricken and shaky. "Moria?" he whispered. "Are you okay?"

Moria pulled her face away from Ramdeo's chest and nodded at Layton, then she turned back. She buried her face once again, her body shaking as she continued to cry.

Right then, Ishaan appeared at the campsite.

"I saw the whole thing from up there," he pointed towards the top platform of a rock formation slightly north of their position. "I was scouting the area on my watch, and I saw Brene go towards Moria's weapon pouch. There's something not right about all this, Layton. She used some high-level magic to get Moria's pouch open. She was trying to kill herself. She tried to cut her wrist, but Moria got up and healed her wound. Then she started saying all these things, almost like she was trying to get Moria to hit her," Ishaan looked down at Brene, unconscious on the ground, blood flowing down out of her nostrils. "She..." He paused for a long while as he studied her.

"She what?" Layton urged.

"She knew things, Layton. Maybe she's been playing with us. Maybe she's known how to use her powers this whole time."

"What things?"

"She knew about Ramdeo and me," Moria wiped her face with the back of her hands, her voice still shaky as she spoke.

"That proves nothing, Moria. You and Ramdeo have been married for almost a decade. Even I've seen you holding hands time and time again. I get it, you don't enjoy displaying affection in the presence of others, but people can pick up on things. You don't have to be sucking face for people to notice that you're a couple."

"She..." Moria swallowed hard. "She said I killed my babies."

She burst out crying, and Ramdeo held her close, rocking her gently and fighting back the tears himself.

Layton walked up to Moria slowly and put a hand on her

shoulder. "You know it wasn't your fault, Moria," Layton closed his eyes and bowed his head. "And you didn't kill your babies."

"You need to stop blaming yourself," Ramdeo wrapped his arms around Moria a little tighter and whispered into her ears. "Even the most mastered witches and warlocks could never prevent a miscarriage. It simply wasn't the will of the universe." Ramdeo allowed a tear to roll down his cheek.

"The inscription," Ishaan whispered, and then hurriedly made his way to his sleeping bag, where he pulled out the piece of parchment on which the map was drawn. He made his way back to the other three and held the parchment open.

"The inscription!" he shouted. "The pure shall come into their power, and spill their own blood on the hour," he readout.

"The pure shall come into their power. Brene... she told me she's still a virgin," Layton said. "Which means she's pure, right?"

"Right! So, she's come into her power... and she's trying to spill her own blood!" Moria exclaimed.

"It must be this place? It has to hold some sort of power that's making her act that way," Ramdeo offered, "How do we stop it?"

"Moria, do you think you could heal her up?" Layton made his way to Brene and crouched down beside her. Wiping her face with her robe, Moria followed. Moria placed her hands above Brene's face, casting a warm light from her palms. Within a few moments, Brene looked to be healed completely.

"I think we should cast a protection spell on her," Layton said, looking up at Ramdeo and Ishaan, who both nodded in agreement.

The four Verdigris sat around Brene's body and gently

placed their hands on her arms' exposed skin. Then they focused their energy, each emitting a different colored light from their palms. For a few moments, there were no sounds in the area except for the buzz from the magic that now surrounded Brene in a multi-colored capsule of sorts, made of ribbons of different colored light. Moria was the first to release Brene's arm, feeling a little drained from healing her as well, followed by Ramdeo, then Ishaan.

"Layton, let the protection spell set," Ishaan said softly. "There's nothing more you can give her right now."

Layton continued to sit in concentration for a few more moments before releasing his grip on Brene's arm and allowing the capsule of magic around her to set.

* * *

BRENE AWOKE SUDDENLY, gasping for breath and whimpering.

"Layton," Moria called. "She's awake."

Moria, Ramdeo, and Ishaan made their way to Brene's sleeping bag, where she was struggling to breathe. Moria took her hand.

"Slowly. Slowly," Moria floated her free hand up and down, breathing in rhythm to the movements. Brene watched closely and followed, eventually feeling relieved at the air entering and leaving her lungs. By the time she had mastered her breathing again, Layton had hurried to her side and looked deep into her eyes.

"Are you okay?" he asked, concerned.

Brene nodded and smiled. "I heard your voice in my head."

Then she turned to Moria, who was still holding her hand.

"Moria," she began, her eyes growing heavy with tears. "I,"

she choked, "I'm so sorry," she squeezed Moria's hand tightly and shook her head. "Those things that I said—"

"It wasn't you, Brene," Moria said kindly, exhaustion in her voice. "It's this place. The magic here is old and cruel." She closed her eyes and shook her head. "I'm the one who should be sorry, I—"

"Don't you dare!" Brene gathered her strength and leaned into Moria, hugging her tenderly and whispering into her ear. "I didn't believe a single thing I was saying, Moria. Not a single thing."

CHAPTER 10

THE REST of the night lasted longer than Brene had ever experienced. As she lay in her sleeping bag, listening to Ishaan's soft snoring nearby, she wished she had never agreed to help the Order. Brene turned over to her side and faced Moria, who was lying on her back, her eyes closed and breathing deeply. Ramdeo had moved his sleeping bag closer to Moria's, and Brene could see their hands intertwined on the dark, dusty floor.

"I can't sleep either," Layton's voice sent a jolt of surprise through Brene's body, causing her to jump a little.

Brene stood up slowly and turned towards the fire around which Layton was sitting, his arms resting on his knees, holding a long stick in his hand with which he was poking the fire.

"Sorry," he said when Brene reached him and took a seat on the ground next to him. "I didn't mean to startle you."

Brene forced a smile and hugged her knees into her chest, absorbing the warmth of the fire. For a long while, the two sat, staring intensely into the fire, until Brene cleared her throat and spoke.

"Thank you," she said, still looking down.

"I did nothing," Layton said, not lifting his eyes from the fire.

"That's not true. You didn't give up on me. I heard your voice." Brene looked up but then dropped her gaze once again when she saw Layton did not lift his eyes to meet hers.

"I don't know how I knew those things," her voice was shaky now. "I can't imagine—" Brene couldn't find the words to say.

"It's your powers," Layton said, finally looking up. "You'll learn to control them."

"I don't want to," Brene whispered, her eyes dazed as if she were lost in deep thought.

The fire crackled in the darkness, and there was a screech in the distance, the sound echoing and bouncing off the rock surfaces. Brene's ears piqued and she frantically scanned the area to locate the source of the sound. When she had located the bird in the distance, perched on a high ledge, she relaxed her body and normalized her breathing.

"Who was it?" Layton asked. Their eyes locked.

"Who was what?" The question confused Brene.

"Who did you drain?"

Brene's eyes widened, and her mouth fell open, her tongue drying as she breathed in the cool air. She forced her lips closed and swallowed hard, and then she wrapped her hands around her body protectively. Brene looked deep into Layton's dark eyes, and in them, she saw something she never really imagined she would. Compassion.

Brene held his gaze until he opened his mouth to speak again, not knowing the words to say.

"For me, it was a Caeruleus in the countryside. I was six. A group of them raided my village, looking for a place to hide from the Order. It was during the civil crisis in the North. My family and I were all in bed by the time the

Caeruleus came to our house. They grabbed my mother and father and slit their throats in front of me." The anger and hurt that he felt could be seen in his eyes. "One man grabbed me by the neck and pulled me out of bed," Layton was squeezing his hands in fists. "They forced me to my knees. Then I reached for his hand, the one that was around the back of my neck. I didn't know why. I just did." He shrugged. "He started to scream loudly. But I felt good. I felt stronger and more powerful than ever. When his corpse fell to the ground, his flesh appearing almost deflated, the rest of his group left screaming an Ipian boy killed the master."

Layton released his hands and placed them back on his knees, wiping the sweat in his palms. Then he turned away from Brene's gaze and looked back into the flames.

"There was a neighboring community of Verdigris that came to our aid. The daughter of the chief saved me and adopted me. Ishaan's her son," Layton smiled to himself. "He welcomed me immediately," he chuckled. "One night, at a feast for the harvest moon, Ishaan introduced me to one of his uncles as his brother. You should have seen the man's face." He shook his head and smiled widely. "Utter confusion."

Brene listened attentively to Layton's story, all the while tightening her embrace on her knees.

"I had found a new family," Layton whispered.

"What about Ramdeo and Moria?" Brene asked, hoping that he wouldn't notice her changing the subject.

"Ramdeo is Ishaan's cousin. His father and our mother are siblings, but his old man died before he was born. Moria and Ramdeo met while they were studying."

"Studying? Does the Verdigris community have schools?"

Layton grunted. "You really think we're barbaric savages, don't you?"

"I didn't mean…," Brene shook her head, then she pulled

her lower lip in, thinking for a long moment before speaking again. "His name was Camdyn." She looked down as she spoke. "He was one of our neighbors back home." She shrugged, releasing her body a little, dropping her hands to rest them on her knees. "I must have been around seven."

Brene could feel her mouth drying, and she struggled to swallow.

"I was helping his wife carry her vegetables home from the market one day. I left them on the table in the kitchen and was about to leave when I heard a door bang. Camdyn was in the kitchen before I knew it. He was drunk. He was screaming at me, asking where I had come from and why I was trying to steal his vegetables. I tried to explain, but he reached for a knife on the counter and came at me. He was so drunk that he fell to the ground, and the knife slid across the kitchen floor, making an awful screeching sound." Brene closed her eyes and shook her head. "I bent down to try to help him up, and when I touched him," Brene shrugged. "I guess all the emotion built up inside me and kind of powered me up. I couldn't control it." She sniffled and wiped her face with the back of her hand before the tears could fall from her heavy eyes.

"How did you feel?" Layton asked. "When you drained him?"

Brene thought for a long moment, trying hard to remember the day she had been banished from her memory so long ago.

"I felt," she began, scrunching her eyebrows before releasing them and allowing the muscles in her face to relax, "different. Like I would never be the same."

Brene had never spoken about any of this before. She had hidden so much of herself for so long that it felt almost therapeutic, sharing these parts of herself with Layton. Somehow, she felt a bond with him, regardless of her initial dislike of how he carried himself. He had saved her, and for that, she was grateful.

"Earlier," Brene began. "When we were at the entrance to the canyon, Moria asked you if you needed some juice. What did she mean?" She looked at him curiously, half knowing the answer to come.

"She offered me some of her life force, her power, to fuel my own abilities," Layton explained.

"Aren't you scared that you'll drain her?" Brene said. Concern evident in her voice.

Layton sighed out. "Brene. What are you doing here?"

The question took Brene by surprise, and she struggled to answer.

"Why did you agree to help the Order? From what I heard from Supreme Pagzman Chahal, it didn't take as much convincing as it took on our side." He raised his eyebrows as he studied her. "You applied to be a part of the Order, what, a dozen times? And they rejected you every time. You know that if you were honest with them about your powers, they would have accepted you without batting an eyelid. So, why lie? Why make yourself seem less than you are?"

Brene listened quietly to Layton's words, all the while holding his gaze, her countenance growing serious.

"You know nothing about me, Layton," Brene finally said, her voice a little colder than necessary, feeling unfairly attacked.

Layton held his hands up in surrender. "I just mean, what's in it for you?"

Brene's expression softened as she thought about the question, then she dropped her head into her hands and sighed loudly. She didn't have an answer. Heck, she'd never even thought about it. She wanted a life of adventure, one where she could make a difference in the world by her actions and work. That's why she wanted to work for the

Order. That was the only way he knew how to make a difference. Maybe she didn't belong here. She was only getting in the way and making things even more difficult for the others. Maybe it was time to go back. Back to her job at Deegan' bar. Back to her credit card debt and overdue bills. Back to being alone. Back to reality.

"You're right, you know," Layton said, his voice warm, softly pulling her from her thoughts with a shrug. "I know nothing about you. Anything worth knowing, anyway." He smirked, sending a jolt through Brene's body and causing her hairs to stand on end.

"On the contrary," Brene's eyes sparkled as she looked at him. "You know more about me than most people do. Goodnight, Layton."

With that, Brene stood and made her way to her sleeping bag, where she tucked herself in and fell into a restful slumber.

* * *

JUST BEFORE DAWN, Brene heard the voice once again. It was piercing and loud, echoing in her head, making it pound and throb, unlike anything she had ever felt before. She sat up in her sleeping bag and held her head in her hands, squeezing her eyes shut and struggling to breathe.

They do not want you to be free, sweet child! The voice was forceful now. You must not let them discourage you. You know what you must do.

"No!" Brene screamed loudly, gripping her head and rocking her body back and forth.

With that, the voice stopped. The sun rose behind the Mountains. Its rays falling down like liquid gold. Brene breathed heavily and looked around her at the others, who were fast asleep. She reached out and touched Moria's arm.

Moria instinctively grabbed Brene's hand and pulled her, causing her to fall forward.

"It's me. Brene," Brene said reassuringly.

"Oh," Moria rubbed her eyes and yawned loudly. "What?" she asked, sleep in her voice.

It was clear to Brene that Moria had returned to her ways, and although her voice was not warm, Brene was grateful that things were back to normal.

"It's sunrise. We should get moving. The sooner we get out of this place, the better." Brene got up and gather the equipment while the rest of the team shook the sleep from their bodies. Her eyes searched for Layton among the group, and when she saw him dusting his sleeping back near the fireplace, she couldn't control the slight smile that appeared on her face.

CHAPTER 11

As they walked through the canyon for the second day in a row, Brene couldn't help but feel uneasy. The rocky features spanning the heights of the canyon walls appeared a dark shade of red compared to the lighter clay color when they had begun their journey. The pace at which they moved was slower and more intentional, each fork in the road causing them to refer to the map until the map no longer served its purpose.

"Look, we've seen these exact rock formations before," Ramdeo pointed upwards towards a ledge that resembled a crocodile's head. "We're going in circles. Ishaan, we need the map."

Ishaan pulled out the map from inside his jacket and laid it on the floor amidst their rocky surroundings. They were in a part of the canyon that was flat, the width seemingly as large as a football field, with no clear vision of an end in sight.

The group huddled around the map, and Moria crouched to the ground and read it. She placed her finger on a few squiggles on the map. "Looks like we're going in the right direction. We should be around here now, which means—"

"Wait a second," Ishaan cut her off. "What's this?"

He pointed at a large image near where Moria's finger landed on the map.

"This wasn't on the map before," he shook his head.

"Some of the ancient maps store more than just the layout of the land," Moria explained. "They could store anything from guardians of sacred grounds or even secret passageways."

She looked up at the rest of the group.

"So, what do you think it is?" Layton asked.

"There's only one way to find out," Moria's eyes darted from one person to another, and then she took a deep breath in and then out gently. She took her hands away from the map and placed them on the ground, dropping one knee to the ground for balance. The dust from the barren ground swirled around her. It formed a whirlwind that looked to be confined to the surrounding space. She stuck her hand out through the dirt particles suspended in the air. Allowing her hand to hover above the image of the owl that appeared on the map.

Moria opened her eyes. The light gray color swirled around her irises like a drop of ink in a body of water. She dropped her gaze to the image of the owl, which suddenly came to life, its head bobbing to the side like a curious child. She mimicked the owl, slowly tilting her head to the side, and the dust particles around her settled back to the ground. Her hand was still hovering above the owl, and the image hopped backward on the map. It screeched loudly; the sound echoing in the empty canyon around them.

Brene's eyes widened at the familiarity of the sound, and she turned her head to Layton, who was so enthralled by what Moria did that he didn't shift his gaze. The image of the owl on the map suddenly spread its wings, screeching angrily at its audience. Moria moved her hand closer to the map, bringing her eyebrows together as she did.

The owl began to beat its wings. Before Moria's hand could make contact with the parchment on which the map was drawn, it flew like an animation off the parchment, its screeches still echoing in the canyon. Moria closed her eyes for a moment and then opened them once again, showing their deep blue color.

"We need to get out of here," Moria said, panic in her voice.

She grabbed the map and stuffed it into Ishaan's hands before making off in a jog towards an area in the canyon walls to their left that appeared to be cave-like. As the team jogged behind Moria, Brene heard the screeches of the owl get louder. She turned her head slightly to see a gigantic bird in the sky above them, hovering like a predator circling its prey.

"Moria," Layton shouted to her. "What did you see?"

"This whole place is cursed," Moria shouted as she ran. "That warning that I read earlier, the one that was making Brene crazy, there's more to it."

"Is that the owl from the map?" Brene screamed, pointing upwards at the bird that the rest of the group didn't seem to see.

"What? Where?" Ramdeo lifted his head as he ran, scanning the skies. "I see nothing."

"What do you mean? It's right there!" There was desperation in Brene's voice now.

The group had broken into a sprint, all of them running as fast as they could towards the canyon wall Moria was leading them to.

"You're the only one who can see it, Brene," Moria shouted. "Look, there's a cave."

She pointed at a small dark hole in the face of the rocky wall ahead, large enough for a baby elephant to fit through.

Brene heard the screeches get louder, and she felt the hair on her hair move in the breeze as the enormous owl swept low. She looked up and locked eyes with the massive beast, its gaze mesmerizing her and causing her to slow her pace until she simply stood looking up.

The owl was a flamboyant teal color. Its feathers resembling the stunning head and chest of a peacock. Its eyes were bright yellow, and its beak a pale purple that matched its large talons and feet. The bird perched itself on a nearby rock and looked deep into Brene's eyes where she stood.

Then Brene dropped to her knees and slowed her breathing. Her mouth fell open as she watched the enchanting creature before her, wondering how soft its feathers must feel.

As she watched the creature before her, silver light engulfed it, flowing around like ribbons in the wind until the creature was no longer there. Instead, in its place, there was a beautiful woman with pale skin and bright yellow eyes, the same color as the owl. Her hair was blonde and fell in long trinkets that reached the ground where she stood, and she was dressed in a glorious silver gown. Around her neck, she wore a teal-colored pendant of an owl, and the smile that she wore on her face seemed fake and misplaced.

"Hello, child," the lady spoke. Her voice was smooth and silvery like that which Brene had heard in her head the day before. "I am the lady of this canyon, Lady Paola." She bowed her head slightly and walked towards Brene.

Brene watched the woman. Her beauty and grace mesmerized her as she sat on her knees a small distance away from the cave in the wall. The lady floating toward her.

Suddenly, Brene's view of the lady was blocked by another figure, standing tall before her, a blade in his hand aimed forward.

"Don't come any closer," Ishaan stood his ground, holding tightly onto the grip of his Katana.

Brene blinked her eyes, feeling dazed and confused, and then she rose slowly. She rubbed her eyes and looked around her, suddenly aware that the rest of the group had taken a protective formation with her in the center. Ishaan stood in front of her, with Layton and Ramdeo on either side and Moria stood beside her with two small blades in each of her hands. Layton held a scabbard in his hands while Ramdeo wrapped the chains of a pair of nunchucks around his left hand.

"What's going on?" Brene looked to Moria for guidance.

"This canyon is cursed. From what I read on the map, the lady of the canyon thrives on the souls of the purebloods who lose their way," Moria spoke hurriedly. "Don't look at her, Brene. Your power gives her power. She's feeding off you."

"Your words are untrue," Lady Paola said, her voice floating through the air like mist. "I simply wish for the pure to be free. But you are different from most, Brenley," she spoke slowly, edging forward slightly.

"Don't move!" Layton screamed.

"It's okay," Moria said. "She can't approach the living. She can't get too close."

"Clever Aligist," Lady Paola chuckled, delight in her voice. "If only you were pure, your soul would bring me much comfort." She lifted her hands in front of her chest and allowed her fingertips to touch, sticking her elbows out as if she were a statue. "I might not be able to approach the living in this form, child, but this is not the only form I take." She smiled eerily and shook her head slowly.

"Brene, close your eyes," Ishaan said. "Put your hands on my shoulders. We'll lead you into the cave."

The lady's gaze fell on Ishaan, an impressed look washing

over her. "Your bloodline is an honorable young man. Why do you risk your life for someone who thinks so little of you?"

"Your words mean nothing to me!" Ishaan yelled. "Move! Now!"

With that, the group jogged towards the cave, Brene closing her eyes all the while. As they moved, so did Lady Paola, although keeping her distance all the while. She floated along gracefully and spoke.

"I have seen her thoughts," she continued. "I have been in her head. She fears you all. She believes you to be primitive savages. Give her to me. Rid yourselves of her."

"That's not true!" Brene screamed as they hurried.

"I have seen what lies in her mind. She would not do the same for you all."

"We're almost there!" Moria reassured them.

"She will only slow you down. Think about it. When has she been of use in this journey so far? She fears her power. She will never use it. She will hold you all back. Bring you all down. Rid yourselves of her."

"She can't leave the canyon. Once we enter the walls, we'll be safe," Moria shouted to the others. "Brene, just keep your eyes closed."

Suddenly, there was a screech in the sky. The lady turned back into an owl, only now the bird looked about the size of an elephant, and the entire group could see it angrily hovering above their heads. The bird screeched loudly, emitting sonic waves from its beak that hit the rock wall ahead, causing large boulders and pieces of the wall to fall to the ground.

"Brene, open your eyes," Ishaan said.

Brene opened her eyes quickly and looked around, allowing her eyes a moment to adjust before moving. The group dodged the falling rocks as they split up and made their way towards the gap in the wall.

"Moria!" Ramdeo's eyes widened as he looked in his lover's direction to see a boulder the size of a house falling to the ground near where she was running.

Just before the boulder could flatten Moria's petite body, a bright green hue of light surrounded her like a shield, causing the boulder to break into a thousand pieces upon contact. Moria looked up at the green bubble of light that had protected her. Then her eyes fell on Brene, who was standing at the entrance to the gap in the wall, her hands extended in Moria's direction and a green mist flowing out of her palms.

"Run!" Brene screamed to Moria, who was the furthest away from the cave-like gap.

The owl's screeches were growing more high-pitched. The sound caused Ishaan, Layton, and Ramdeo to press their palms hard against their ears, screaming in agony as the piercing sounds caused blood to flow from their ears down their necks. The three men made their way to the cave and thrust themselves in, panting as they lay on the dark ground, grateful to be out of harm's way.

"Moria!" Ramdeo got to his feet and stood next to Brene at the cave entrance, and then his eyes were drawn back up into the sky.

"Um… Brene," he said slowly, nudging her.

The owl had grown to the height of a 20-story building. Making its way towards them, holding large boulders in its beak that it was throwing in their direction, making the ground shake around them.

Brene reached the gap in the wall and thrust herself in just in time as the owl threw a large boulder that sealed the entrance of the cave, missing Moria's body by an inch.

CHAPTER 12

IT WAS pitch black in the cave once the boulder sealed the entrance, and the sound of rocks falling and breaking away from the wall still echoed through the cave walls. Brene sat on the cold floor and breathed heavily, listening closely to the surrounding sounds, feeling the ground shake beneath her and the walls shake. She could hear Moria breathing beside her and Layton and Ishaan whispering nearby. Ramdeo was the first to speak.

"Moria! Are you okay?" he asked, his voice shaky as though he'd been crying.

"I'm alright," Moria replied, sniffling a little. "Brene? Are you okay?"

Brene slowly moved her arms and touched her head, face, shoulders, and legs, ensuring she couldn't feel any blood. Then she moved her legs a little to make sure that none of them were injured.

"I'm alright," she said. "Can anybody see anything?"

"There's a light further in," Layton said. "I can see it."

"He's right," Ishaan concurred. "There's a light, but I can't see anything else."

Brene heard a long, hard breath and felt warmth in the air around her, and then a light appeared, glowing brighter as time passed. Ramdeo held his hands to his mouth and blowing into them, the power from his breath causing a ball of light to form in his hands. He held the ball of light in his hands as he lowered them to chest level and made his way towards Moria first.

Brene watched as he looked at her, tears pooling in his eyes. Moria caressed his face as she allowed a tear to escape from her own eye. Then, Ramdeo turned away from her and moved slowly to illuminate as much of the cave as possible.

As Ramdeo moved, Brene could make out two figures that she identified as Ishaan and Layton. She moved towards them instinctively, and Moria followed.

"When did you learn how to do that?" Layton asked Brene, looking proud and impressed all at once.

"Maybe I can teach you sometime. If you can teach me how to control my other powers," she smiled, and Layton chuckled and nodded.

Ramdeo gently lifted his arms high above his head, pushing the floating sphere of light upwards. Then he cast an ancient spell by chanting in a strange language that Brene had never heard before. Once he had done with his incantation, the sphere of light moved as if it had a mind of its own. It pushed its way past Ishaan and Layton and lit the pathway ahead, leading the way as the group followed.

Ishaan followed first behind the sphere of light, followed by Ramdeo, Moria, Brene, and Layton. They continued to walk deep into the cave; the air growing colder as they did and darkness following close by.

"Brene," Moria said quietly as they reached a slightly wider area and could walk side-by-side.

"Don't even mention it," Brene held her gaze and smiled

warmly. "We're even now." She raised her eyebrows, and Moria returned her smile.

They walked for hours through the dark caves that went deep into the canyon walls until they saw a light at the end of their path. The sphere of light that Ramdeo had conjured dissolved into the air, and they slowly made their way towards the natural light. When they reached the end of their path, their eyes opened wide in wonder and pleasant surprise as they slowly left the cave and entered a massive water hole.

The cave exit was leveled with the land covered in grass and the roots of trees, intertwined between them for stability. There were tall trees all around, as well as short shrubs and bushes. A few yards away was a large water hole with one half completely covered in water lilies and the other uncovered. The crystal clear water was in constant motion due to the life that was all too present at that moment. Humongous hippos and their cubs stood in the shallows in one area, only their snouts visible above the surface. Elephants trumpeted happily as they sprayed water at each other. Crocodiles sunbathed on the banks, their mouths gaping open to allow for the birds to peck at the leftovers in their teeth. On the other side of the water hole, the air seems to sparkle and shine, causing a buzzing in Brene's stomach, warming her from the inside out.

They walked forward and made their way through a few trees, ensuring that the trees hid their bodies so that the animals did not see them. They stood behind some bushes on a little hill near the water hole and looked down.

"There's magic here," Brene said. "I can feel it."

"Me too," Layton said.

"Pixies," Moria said, nodding across the water hole. "Maybe we could use some of their power to find a way out of here."

"How do you suppose we do that?" Ishaan turned to the rest of the group.

"They aren't amiable creatures," Brene added. "And from what I'm feeling, there's a lot of magic in this place."

"She's right," Ramdeo agreed. "They're probably practicing dark magic. Let's look at the map again."

"It's not complete," Moria said.

Ishaan and Layton turned away from the water hole and faced Moria, frowns painted on both their faces.

"What do you mean?" Layton asked.

"The map. It's not complete. This was all part of some bigger plan. The Order wanted us to get lost in the canyon." Moria removed her cloak and sat on the floor, and then she sat down on it and crossed her legs, resting her hands on her knees with her palms facing the sky in meditation. "Sit down," she ordered.

Layton, Ishaan, and Ramdeo sat down on the surrounding ground, and the four Verdigris each made the edge of a square.

"You too, Brene," Moria looked at Brene, still standing by the bush and watching the pixies across the river. They seemed to throw something around, like a sort of game. Brene reluctantly turned her focus away from the pixies and sat on the ground, shifting the rest so that the five made a circle.

"I have to show you what I saw when I read the map," Moria said, holding Brene's gaze with compassion in her eyes.

Brene felt the focus fall on her as she looked around the circle.

"Is it about me?" she asked. "Is it why the lady affected me so much? And why the protection spell you cast didn't work?" She blinked.

Moria nodded and closed her eyes. "Take each other's

hands." They did as Moria instructed. "Now, close your eyes, and whatever you do, don't open them until I say so."

Brene closed her eyes and heard Moria chanting. The words sounded like a symphony of sounds that lingered around in the air. Making her feel like she was floating. Her eyes were closed, but there was a light in her vision. A bright white light was swallowing her whole as she drifted to the sounds of Moria's chanting.

Suddenly, the bright light changed, and Brene felt like she was back on the other side of the great canyon wall. She saw the image of the owl before her on the parchment, bobbing its head to the side playfully. She was the only one in the canyon, holding the map in her hands and trying to make sense of the images. Then, around the owl, inscriptions appeared in a language that she couldn't quite make out. The owl spoke, but it was not in the lady's voice that had lingered in her head before. It was the voice of a man. A kind and warm voice that comforted her and made her feel safe.

"How have you come to possess this map?" the owl asked as it bobbed its head. "You do not look like someone I have known."

Brene moved closer to the owl, surprise washing over her.

"Never mind now. You are in grave danger. You must leave this place. This canyon is cursed. There is a Lady, the Lady Paola, a great shape-shifter queen that was banished to these lands many eons ago. She was the wife of the great leopard shape-shifter whose soul was banished into the Myxan. You must go. She will corrupt the minds of the pure and cause them to shed their own blood. She will take their souls as her own, for she has one goal and one goal only."

"What's that?" Brene asked.

"To become the Pure Bride," the owl whispered. "I will show you."

"I don—"

Before Brene could complete her thought, the scene before her changed again, and she was whisked away to a world altogether unfamiliar. She was in the middle of a clearing, blankets of snow all around her. At the dead center of the clearing was a pedestal made of charcoal-gray stone.

Brene walked towards the pedestal and brushed the snow off the top surface, exposing an engraving on the slab.

The concord inscribed will bring by false peace
As cozenage and truth engulfs all you know
The hate and the darkness will only increase
The heat of the great orb melting the snow
Dark magic shall burgeon and fill up the air
And the Cursed One will rise to take up great reign
His power and ardor beyond all compare
With his Pure Bride beside him bringing discord and pain
For the Cursed One to reign in this time and beyond
On the night of the blood moon, the two souls must bond.

Brene read the words engraved on the stone carefully. She recognized the first few lines as the prophecy of the Myxan. So she realized that what she was looking at was the complete prophecy, which the Grand Master of the Redgarde cult did not complete at the time of his execution.

Brene read the prophecy once more and committed the words to memory before looking around. She suddenly felt cold and wrapped her arms around her shoulders, breathing deeply and watching the mist her breath made in the cold.

Now what? She thought. Am I stuck here?

"What happens next, owl?" Brene screamed into the trees surrounding the glade as she spun on her heel. She knew she would die of frostbite if she stood out there any longer. So she made her way towards the forest in the Westerly direction to the glade. As she hiked through the forest, she couldn't help but wonder where the rest of the group was. She hoped they were alright.

After trekking through the forest for a couple miles, Brene came across a cabin in the middle of the woods that seemed to stand alone amidst the trees. There were no other cabins in the general vicinity, and Brene saw the light of a fire burning through the window. Thank goodness! Brene thought. She made her way towards the window and looked into the cabin.

Inside, on the back of the door, Brene saw two long black coats hanging, and on the rug before the fire, a young lady was sitting and reading a book. In a rocking chair nearby, a middle-aged woman rocked as she knitted, talking all the while. On the table closest to the window outside which Brene stood, there were weapons laid out. A few words, some axes, and a dozen small daggers.

From where Brene stood, she could hear what the two women chatted about, and so she moved her face a little closer to the window and listened attentively.

"Do you know your role, Nirmala?" the middle-aged woman asked.

"Yes, mother, I know my role. We've been over it a million times." Nirmala put her book down on the floor and turned, gently placing her hands on her mother's lap. "Don't worry," she smiled. "And it's just the two of us around. You don't have to call me that. You can call me by my real name."

The young lady got up off the floor and fetched a black teapot she hooked on a metal rod suspended slightly above the fire.

"Tea, mother?" she asked.

"But you're sure you understand the plan." Her mother looked worried. "If anything happens, you know where to meet me? At the—"

"The riverside inn on the other side of the frozen river. Past the Grayfair Village and over the hill. I'll be fine."

"I know," the middle-aged woman looked to be fighting tears. "It's just. It's such a big task. If you're not up for it, you can be honest with me. We can find someone else."

The woman closed her eyes and shook her head slowly.

"Mother, I'll be fine." The young lady made her way back to her mother and sat on the floor, resting her head in her mother's lap. "The Myxan has to be destroyed. We've worked too hard for too long to let the darkness destroy this world."

The middle-aged woman put her knitting aside and placed her hands on her daughter's head, lovingly stroking her hair as her eyes filled with tears. "They will write songs about your great sacrifice, my darling. They will remember you as the one who stopped the darkness from consuming us. Brenley, the hero of the free world."

Brene's eyes widened in shock, and her heart began to beat fast in her chest, making her stomach churn and her head pound. She remembered the words of Supreme Pagzman Chahal.

One should never forsake the name of one's ancestor. Was this her ancestor? But the woman, she called her daughter Nirmala. Why does that name sound so familiar? Many thoughts floated around Brene's mind, each giving rise to new questions but no answers. Then the scene changed once more.

Brene found herself in a different part of what seemed like the same forest. She heard voices in the distance and ran in their direction, hugging her body as she did, trying hard to brace herself against the cold. She reached the end of the forest, a large sheet of ice lying before her, under which she could see water flowing freely. She saw a young man in the distance, holding a bundle in his hand, and the lady called Nirmala.

She's the Nirmala from the Myxan lore. Brene stood frozen at the realization. She was the descendant of the right hand to the head of the Redgarde cult. Only, it seemed like Nirmala was a double agent of sorts. She intended to destroy the Myxan all along. Brene was suddenly aware of her vigorous shivering, forcing herself to drop to the ground and hug her knees into her chest. Then, once again, the scene before her changed.

She was no longer in a forest but in a meadow. The air was warm and inviting, and the smell of fresh flowers lingered all around. Brene breathed in the sweet air greedily, stretching out her arms and absorbing the warmth into her body. Once she felt warm and comfortable once again, she turned around to assess her surroundings.

Behind her was a wall made of tiny pebbles that seemed to go on forever in either direction. It was as tall as her hip and seemed very easy to hop over. Brene walked towards the wall slowly and placed her hands on it, feeling the warmth that the stones offered her. She walked along the wall, running her hand along the smooth pebbles as she did until she heard a few hushed voices ahead. She jumped over the wall and ducked down just as two tall individuals approached.

One was a strapping man with piercing eyes and a muscular physique, and his arm was intertwined with a woman. As soon Brene laid eyes on the woman's face, her heart beat hard once again, and she felt her palms become clammy. It was the Lady Paola from the canyon.

"If your family is not happy with our alliance, then perhaps we should run away," Lady Paola said, sounding sad and desperate.

"My love," the man said. "I love you with all that I am, and to you, I shall always belong. Our love shall be consummated, that I promise you. All I ask is for your patience. I have found a way for us all to live happily."

"How?" Lady Paola asked.

"That is why I have brought you here. I wanted you to be the first other to experience life over the wall with me. It is truly glorious, my love. You'll see."

Brene sat crouched behind the wall, and then suddenly, there was light all around her once again. She felt as though she was floating and slowly descending back to the Earth. She heard a familiar voice and followed the sound.

"You may open your eyes," Moria's voice was soft and meditative as she guided them out of their visions.

Brene opened her eyes and allowed them a moment to adjust to their surroundings. Then she looked over her shoulder and through a gap in between the trees to make sure that they were still alone and that the pixies had not sensed their presence.

After seeing them continue to throw something around, she turned back to the group, who were all rubbing their eyes and yawning widely.

"What the fuck?" Brene said, and from the silence and slow nods that followed, she trusted everyone felt the same.

CHAPTER 13

THEY SAT in silence for a moment as everyone absorbed the scenes from the visions that they had just experienced.

"I still don't understand," Brene said, looking around the circle frantically. "I'm the descendant of the right hand of the Redgarde cult leader. So what? That means nothing."

She stared deeply into Moria's eyes, conveying a feeling of emptiness in her own.

"Does it?" she asked softly.

"The lore," Layton began, with a kindness in his voice as if he were talking to a little child. "Was written a long time ago by a Freedom Fighter. He committed the events of the dark times to parchment, which became our world's history. But like any story, Brene, there's more than one side."

"So, the lore is a lie?" Brene asked matter-of-factly.

Ishaan smiled and let out a large puff of air through his nose. "It's just one perspective of what really happened," he shrugged.

"So, what really happened?" Brene was surprised at the urgency in her own voice. For so long, she had felt so lost in the world. And now, in all the chaos and uncertainty, as strange as it seemed, she felt found.

Moria sighed loudly and shared a look with her fellow Verdigris. Then she held Brene's gaze. "The Freedom Fighters were not the only ones who believed that the power of the Myxan did not belong in this world. The Verdigris believed so as well." She paused, looking around the circle. "Nirmala, the right hand of the head of the Redgarde cult, was a Verdigris."

Brene's eyes widened as she listened to Moria's tale.

"Verdigris believe that all magic should be practicable. It should be our right as those who have magic in our blood to choose what magic we want to practice. But even within our community, there is division. Some choose to practice a dark type of magic, like those who sacrifice their own kin for unnatural powers. But some practice with light and care, not intending to harm or gain power for themselves." She nodded at her friends.

"I thought Verdigris practiced magic beyond the legal regulations," Brene said.

"We do," Ramdeo explained. "But there are so many ways to practice magic that they all can't be regulated by law. Verdigris became branded as outcasts when the government found out that we were casting spells in groups. Something as silly and trivial as that," He scoffed. "There aren't any laws regulating the use of magic in groups to create a multi-source of power."

Brene scrunched her eyebrows hard, and then her forehead relaxed as the realization settled within her.

"So, you don't practice dark magic?" she asked curiously.

"Not particularly, no," Layton shrugged. "We just practice magic that isn't regulated by law. Mostly group magic and drawing power from a few animals. Our elders had appealed to the government hundreds of times, requesting that laws be included to regulate Verdigris practices as well. They even requested a member of our community to sit as a silent party in the elections. But the narrative that we were outcasts who sacrificed our children played into the Order's plans, I guess."

"That's why we're here," Ishaan lifted his knees a little and hugged them loosely. "The three Supreme Pagzmans agree that Verdigris practices should be regulated by law as well. So, they are working on drafting the regulations. We're working for them in return."

"So, what happens then?" Brene asked.

"It would make life easier," Ramdeo shrugged. "Less unemployment, greater living conditions, things like that."

Brene suddenly felt her stomach drop at the thought of her judgments towards the four Verdigris.

"I'm sorry. I didn't know." She looked down and shook her head.

"You couldn't have known, Brene," Moria reached out and touched her leg. "So, the Verdigris wanted to destroy the Myxan just as much as the Freedom Fighters, but they had the advantage of actually practicing magic that was somewhat unregulated. So, many of them joined the Redgarde cult undercover to familiarize themselves with the ins and outs of the area and how the cult functioned. Legend has it; there were four Verdigris at that battle. In the chaos of it all, they killed at least a dozen Redgarde cult members before being killed by the Freedom Fighters."

"Why isn't all of this in the lore?" Brene asked, feeling a wave of anger grow within her at learning that the Order had hidden so much of the truth from the world.

"The Order doesn't care much for the truth," Layton spat, the disgust clear in his voice.

"But the Supreme Pagzmans—"

"The Supreme Pagzmans are merely puppets, Brene," Ramdeo explained, sadness in his voice. "They're the face of the Order. They don't make the rules or executive decisions. They're just as trapped as we are in the greater scheme of things."

Brene's head was hurting from all the new information. The Supreme Pagzmans weren't the actual leaders of the Order. She was the descendant of a Verdigris warrior. She had entered the Redgarde cult undercover and had climbed the ranks to the leader's right hand. The lore was all lies. Brene dropped her head down into her hands and sighed out loudly.

"Okay. So, what happened to Nirmala?" Brene asked, slowly raising her head.

"Some Freedom Fighters killed her in the battle. The one who had stolen the Myxan." Moria explained. "But legend has it, she had birthed a son many years before, and he lived in a Village with his father."

"So, I'm her descendant." Hearing the words out loud sent a jolt of energy through Brene's body.

The others nodded at her.

"What about Lady Paola? And the prophecy? Did you see it too?" Her eyes darted among them. "It was engraved on that big rock in the middle of the glade." She held her hands out, trying to mimic the size of the stone pedestal.

"I don't understand," Layton said. "So, Lady Paola was the great shape-shifter's lover. But there wasn't anything about her in Verdigris lore either."

"At least we have the full prophecy," Ramdeo said, nodding. "That'll make the Order happy."

"I don't understand either. Layton's right. There's no mention of her anywhere. I don't know exactly what's going on," Moria said. "But I know how to get the complete story," she said triumphantly.

"How?" Despite being uncomfortable and lost in the middle of nowhere, excitement was flowing through Brene like she had never felt before.

"I need to speak to the owl." She held her hands out for the map, which Ishaan pulled out from inside his jacket and placed in her hands. She took a deep breath in and sighed it out. "I need to use Nedeaubre."

She looked around at the others.

Ishaan stood up quickly and took a step back as if Moria had spoken unspeakable words. Brene watched his eyes grow wide with horror, and his body became stiff and agitated.

"There has to be another way," he shook his head frantically.

Brene turned her focus to Layton and Ramdeo, who looked equally shocked as Ishaan, and stared hard at Moria.

"Is there another way?" Ramdeo asked; his voice shaky and low.

Moria shook her head slowly, a look of helplessness washing over her.

"We don't need to find out now." Brene's eyes darted from one person to another. There was obviously something sinister about what Moria was suggesting. "Maybe we can conjure a portal to take us back home. Then we can reassess the situation. I mean, we've got a lot from this expedition already. We have the entire prophecy now, for goodness' sake."

"A portal would draw too much attention." Layton shook his head. "The last thing we need is dark pixies draining us of our magic."

Ishaan was pacing behind the group now, contributing significantly to the tension in the air around.

"Ishaan," Moria said calmly. "We won't do it unless you're okay."

Brene studied the others carefully and decided that it would be best not to ask too many questions at this time.

Ishaan stopped pacing and faced the group.

"Do you need me?" he asked, his eyes swelling with tears. Brene had never seen the man look quite so defeated.

Layton and Ramdeo stood slowly and dusted the grass from their bottoms, and then they turned towards their friend and smiled warmly. "You don't have to," Layton put a brotherly hand on his shoulder. "Looks like..," he turned back to Brene. "We have a spare Verdigris for cases such as these."

Brene looked up from where she was sitting. She swallowed hard before speaking. "What is it, exactly, that we're going to do?"

"Nedeaubre, is dark prohibited magic. Some Verdigris practice the dark arts, and the power that fuels them becomes addictive. Ishaan lost himself down that path before," Moria whispered to Brene as Ramdeo and Layton comforted Ishaan a small distance away. "In the same way that an Ipian becomes power hungry when they feed off another, practicing dark magic makes you lose your sense of reality. All you see is power. All you need is power."

A sad look washed over Moria's face.

"Ishaan," she thought a long while before continuing. "He meant well. He always meant well." Tears pooled in her eyes, "But we all have darkness inside. And if you don't keep that darkness at bay, it consumes you."

Brene listened hard, a shiver running through her body at the thought of draining another's power and craving more. She felt her chest grow tight as she breathed. Each exhale shakier than the last. Moria swallowed hard and shook her head as if to displace the thoughts settling in her mind. Then she stood up, dusted the grass off her body, and ushered Brene to do the same.

She felt fear inside her growing rapidly as she slowly stood and looked around. A buzzing in her head seemed to grow louder by the second. The surrounding air appeared hazy.

"We're going to have to make a sacrifice," Moria shouted so that the men could hear as well.

Brene felt a surge of intensity run through her body, fear and anxiety hovering over her like a cloud.

"S-sacrifice?" Brene asked, trying hard to mask how scared she felt. "A-a dark magic sacrifice?"

She swallowed hard again. Brene brought her hand up to her chest and clenched her shirt in her fist. She was struggling to breathe now.

Layton hurried to her and placed his hand over hers on her chest. He put his other hand on her shoulder and looked deep into her eyes.

"It's okay. Breathe," he breathed deeply, and Brene followed suit, slowing her breathing down. "That's it."

As he breathed in, he lifted his head, and as he breathed out, he bowed gently. The warmth of his hand on hers made Brene feel safe, and she edged her body closer to him, allowing his warmth to wrap around her.

"We're not sacrificing you," Layton chuckled. "Relax. It's an animal sacrifice." He smiled warmly.

Brene breathed out deeply, relief in her countenance. She felt a little silly that she thought that they would sacrifice a human at all. After all, she had grown to care for each group member dearly, and she knew in her heart that they were good people. Moria, Ramdeo, and Ishaan shared a look, and then they all grinned widely.

"You thought we were going to sacrifice you?" Ramdeo asked, his eyes gleaming. "Hah! You really do think we're all just primitive savages, don't you?" he chuckled.

Brene felt the blood rush to her face quickly. She opened her mouth to speak, thinking hard of the words to say when Ramdeo continued. "You're lucky we like you, Brene." He held out his index finger and waved it in her direction, wearing a warm smile. "You're forgiven this time."

Brene's body eased a little, and her face drained some of its red color. She smiled back at Ramdeo gratefully, a look of admiration on her face. Just then, she realized that Layton's hand was still on hers, and she was so close to him that she could feel his breath on her skin. She jumped back abruptly and swallowed hard.

"Thank you," she said; her voice still a little shaky and her blood boiling from the physical chemistry.

Layton smirked, his piercing eyes holding her gaze, only this time there was a hunger in them that Brene had never seen before. The need caused her skin to tingle and heat to rush down between her legs.

"Uh... guys?" Ishaan was facing away from them and towards the watering hole. "You might want to reconsider your plan."

The rest of the group rushed towards him, looking over the bush that concealed them earlier. There, before them, was the water hole, only there was not a single living soul in sight.

"What? Where did they all go?" Ramdeo frantically scanned the area.

"We need to get out of this place." Layton stared at the empty water hole. "I guess it's time for Plan B."

"What—" Brene began, but was cut off before she could completely express herself.

Layton turned around swiftly and placed his hands on Brene's hips, and then he pulled her closer and gently pressed his lips against hers. Although her first instinct was to pull away defiantly, she couldn't stop herself from leaning in and feeling his warmth against her skin. Brene closed her eyes and felt his hands on her, her body thrusting forwards slightly at his touch. She opened a mouth and allowed his tongue to massage hers, moaning as heat pulsated through her body. She lifted her hands that were hanging limply at her sides and placed her hands on Layton's chest, feeling his heart beating just as quick as hers. She felt power surging through her body as Layton kissed her harder and with more passion. Then he slowed down and pulled his face away from hers.

Brene stood for a moment with her eyes closed, panting and feeling more alive than she had ever before. She slowly opened her eyes and looked straight ahead at Layton, who was smiling widely.

Suddenly, she felt a buzzing in her hands, and she pulled her gaze away from Layton's piercing eyes. She lifted her hands to eye level and gasped in surprise at her glowing fingers and palm. Her hands glowed a bright green color. The same as the bubble she created earlier, only now, the power looked less refined and more as though she was an open circuit, spitting out electricity. The bright green light from her hands reflected in her eyes as well. They turned to a shade of green similar to that of a meadow after a week of rain.

Layton held his hands up in front of him, his palms facing Brene.

"Breathe," he said supportively. "You need to refine the power." He raised his eyebrows, his piercing eyes now sparkling with pride. "Just breathe," he said slowly.

Brene followed his instructions and focused on her breath, all the while watching her hands. As she breathed, the electricity-like appearance of the green light in which her hands were soaked slowly smoothed out until her hands themselves were glowing the same green as her eyes.

"What did you do?" Brene asked softly, mesmerized by the color of her hands and studying them. Her eyes were wide and emotionless now, the power in her hands making her feel alive and absorbing all her focus.

"Brene," Layton's voice broke her deep concentration, and she blinked for the first time since she laid eyes on her hands, still unable to look away. "Don't let the power get the better of you. I need you to find a way out," he spoke slowly, encouraging her with care and support. "Nod your head if you can hear me."

There was a loud buzzing in Brene's ears, causing Layton's voice to sound muffled and far away. She nodded slowly.

"Good. Good. Now, I need you to find a way out of here. Nod if you understand." Layton's voice sounded further away now.

Brene nodded. She closed her eyes and allowed the buzzing in her ears to engulf all other sounds around her. Then she turned her hands so that her palms were facing the ground and slowly crouched down. She placed her palms on the ground. The trees around her rustled in a wind that seemed to originate from Brene herself. Her hands glowed brighter as she pushed them deeper into the ground, and she felt little vines coming from the earth and gently caressing her palms.

"Which way?" she whispered to the vines.

The ground beneath them shook. Crackling filled the air as the roots of the surrounding trees scurried, laying themselves in two parallel lines to form a path just to the group's right.

Brene dropped her knees to the ground. Lowered her head so that her lips were close to the soil. "Thank you," she whispered to the vines underneath her hands.

Just then, bright yellow and purple flowers bloomed on

the roots that had surfaced and formed the pathway. Brene opened her eyes and stood up slowly, turning to face the path. She smiled widely at the sight of the flowers, and a tear fell down her cheek as she chuckled.

She whipped her head back towards Layton. "You let me feed off your power." She was still smiling widely, her eyes gleaming from the tears that were accumulating. "And I didn't drain you," she laughed, a look of amazement on her face.

"Don't get too cocky, Ipian," Moria teased and patted her on the back, smiling widely as well. "But nice job."

"Get down!" Ramdeo whispered loudly. "I hear something."

They all frantically dropped to the ground, and Brene looked around, swiftly moving her head from side to side. They were still and quiet. Except for the sound of the rustling of the leaves, not even a breath could be heard.

"Sorry," Ramdeo stood up. "I thought I—"

Masked men suddenly appeared from behind a nearby bush, holding scabbards and spears in their hands. There were a dozen men and they circled the group quickly, creating no room for escape and little for a fight.

One man, dressed quite like a pirate with large gold earrings and a white beard, stepped towards Brene. Still, before he could reach her, Layton jumped in the way, pulling his Katana from its sheath and aiming the blade at their attacker. The pirate smiled widely, showing an upper jaw, somewhat like an old piano with a discerning pattern of black and off-white teeth.

The pirate slowly lifted an empty hand to mouth level and blew hard, causing a whirlwind of sand to surround them all.

"Take them all!" A deep, hoarse voice croaked loudly.

Brene looked around frantically, screaming Layton's

name, but the whirling sound of the surrounding sand drowned all else out. She felt something hard hit the back of her head, and her knees gave way, dropping her body to the ground. She blinked, trying hard to see through the flying sand, and then once again, darkness engulfed her.

CHAPTER 14

BRENE OPENED HER EYES, her vision blurry and unfocused. She slowly lifted her head and tried to steady herself, feeling a pounding behind her eyes affecting her balance. She lifted her hand to touch her head and felt the sudden cold resistance of a chain. She was chained.

She sat up frantically and looked around, then looked down at her hands. There were thick black metal chains around each of her wrists. The other end was attached to the bed on which she was lying. She appeared to be in a large tent of sorts. The ground was covered in layers of rugs and carpets. Towards the sides of the tent, there were shelves of books and ornaments. The bed on which she was sitting was on the far side of the tent. Directly across from her was the entrance. A slit in the cream-colored fabric of which the shelter was made. The material was drawn apart like the drapes of a curtain. Outside, the sun seemed to be shining brightly.

Brene closed her eyes tightly and tried to harness power. For a moment, her hands glowed green, and the chains trembled, but it was of little use. She was not strong enough.

"There are some pretty heavy containment spells on those."

The sudden appearance of a deep voice caused Brene to jump with fright. She followed the sound of the voice to the corner of the tent to her right. A young man sat in a large armchair. His elbows resting on the armrests. His fingers of each hand coming together in front of his chest, his hands forming somewhat of a cage. The man had dark brown hair tied in a knot at the base of his head and matched his facial hair. His face was handsome and his dark brown eyes piercing, a countenance of seriousness plainly displayed. On the middle finger of his left hand, he wore a bulky metal ring that looked to be made of five circles of equal size. One in the middle and four around it. Each touching the other only on the circumference; never overlapping or interlacing. He wore dark leather pants that matched his waistcoat, under which he wore a cream-colored, loose-fitting shirt. His boots, although dark brown, had splashing of a dark brown-red color, which Brene thought looked very much like dried blood.

Brene watched the strange man closely, her eyes focused and her senses on edge.

"I can help you take them off," the man said, and then he called out loudly to someone outside the tent.

The white-haired man with large gold earrings that Brene had met earlier entered the tent, holding two men by their necks. Both men were stripped down to their underwear and wore a sack on their heads. Their hands were secured with dark black metal chains like those around her own wrist, and their bodies displayed long slashes out of which blood was dripping and oozing. The white-haired man kicked them both, forcing them to fall onto their knees, and pulled off the sacks on their head.

Brene's eyes widened in horror as she saw Ramdeo's face,

his eyes blue and swollen and his mouth covered in blood. Brene watched him struggle to keep his eyes open, his body swaying as he collapsed forwards, and coughing blood on the carpet.

The other man kneeling on the floor, Brene had not seen before. He was slightly built, with bright yellow hair and blue eyes. His face was equally puffy as Ramdeo's, but his left ear was severed off his head, the blood dripping down his neck.

"Get up!" The white-haired man kicked Ramdeo in the gut, causing him to fall onto his side.

Brene jumped up and rushed forward, but the chains hindered her movement. "Get the fuck away from him!"

She pulled at the chains, each effort causing her hands to glow bright green.

"That's it. Get angry." The man in the room's corner continued to sit as he was, watching the scene before him and smiling.

Brene turned to him, fire in her eyes and heart, and held his gaze.

"What do you want?" she yelled. Her throat hurting at the force of her words.

"I want you to break out of your chains, Brenley," the man's voice was as cold and emotionless as his countenance. "Drain them."

Brene could feel her pupils dilate as her eyes widened further, her nostrils flaring in anger.

"Never," she spat.

"Perhaps you do not understand the situation, Brenley. Let me simplify it for you. Either you drain them and break out of your chains, or Quick here is going to slit their throats."

Brene opened her mouth to speak, but she did not know the words to say. A look of disgust washed over her as she held the man's gaze. The man lifted his right hand and motioned to Quick, who grabbed the men by their hair and dragged them forward so that they were within Brene's reach. Brene looked down at Ramdeo and the other man, both lying on the ground, unable to stand, and she tried her hardest to hide the fear she felt.

"Please," she whispered, her gaze still on Ramdeo. "Please don't make me." She closed her eyes and shook her head. "I can't."

"If you can't, then your friends die, Brenley."

Ramdeo moaned, and Brene gasped. She crouched down and spoke fast. "Ramdeo? Can you hear me?" Brene heard the shakiness in her own voice and swallowed hard.

Ramdeo groaned and coughed, splashing more blood onto the carpet. He breathed in deeply and coughed again.

"Moria," he whispered, struggling to speak. "Save Moria."

"Shut the fuck up!" Quick stepped forward and kicked Ramdeo in his gut once again.

Suddenly, Brene grabbed his leg. "I said, get the fuck away from him!" Her eyes glowed green as she spoke, and the white-haired man screamed in agony, unable to move his body.

His eyes widened, and his jaw fell. The pain was clear on his face as he screamed. Brene's eyes glowed brighter as she drained the man of his power, her veins becoming visible through her skin as the power she absorbed flowed through them. As the man wasted away, Brene breathed in deeply, the power inside her growing and healing her entirely. She released her grip on the man and closed her eyes. Brene closed her hands tightly into fists, shattering the shackles around her wrists into millions of tiny pieces.

She kicked aside the lifeless corpse of the man that she had drained and turned to the man sitting in the corner. He smiled at her widely as she walked towards him, then clapped slowly as he stood.

"Excellent, Brenley," he said.

"Let us go," Brene said slowly, her eyes still glowing bright green.

The man chuckled. "Now, why would I do that? I've been waiting for you for centuries." He reached for an apple that sat on a shelf nearby. "Here. You must be starved."

Brene pounced forward, placing her hands on the man's wrists and trying hard to drain him of his power, but the man simply stood before her, smiling widely. Brene saw a bright orange color flicker through his dark brown eyes as the energy drained from her and entered his body. Brene gasped for breath as she felt herself weakening, then she fell to the ground unconscious.

CHAPTER 15

BRENE SAT up suddenly and found herself in the same tent in which she awoke earlier. Now, however, her hands were not bound in chains, and there was no one sitting in the corner, watching her every move. Brene got to her feet, and her eyes dropped to the stains of blood on the floor that Ramdeo had made earlier. Panic filled her body as she ran towards the entrance of the tent and slowly peered out.

Outside, it was no longer day. The sky was a deep shade of blue, slowly turning to black. Brene stuck her head out of the tent and looked around. There were people all about, some around fires chatting happily, and others walking about.

Brene stepped outside. The men and women around her stopped what they were doing, fell to their knees, and bowed their heads. Then in unison, they chanted, "Hail the Pure Bride!" before standing up and continuing with their tasks.

All around, Brene saw tents similar to that which she had just stepped out of. At the tops of the tents were flags on which the same symbol as that on the man's ring was painted. The five circles only touching at their circumferences, never overlapping or intertwining. Like an army preparing for war, the tents continued for as far as Brene could see in each direction.

Suddenly, the men and women around stopped in their tracks, once again, fell down to their knees, and chanted, "Hail the Cursed One!" once again, then stood and continued their tasks.

"Please, come inside," the man from earlier appeared to her left and held the tent open. "I'll explain everything."

He smiled, although Brene did not sense any warmth or kindness about the man.

Brene stood for a long time, holding the man's gaze until he eventually spoke again. "If you run, my men will cut you down, and I will kill your friends," the man said in a matter-of-fact tone.

"How do I know they're still alive?" Brene asked, finding her courage once again.

"Very well." The man released the opening of the tent and walked past Brene. "Follow me."

Brene followed the man close behind. As they walked through the crowds, every man and woman bowed their heads towards them, as though they were royalty stepping out of their palace and gracing the world with their presence.

The man led Brene through a maze of tents, each area looking almost identical to the last. Brene couldn't help but think how difficult it would be to escape from her captor should she find her friends no longer alive. The entire place was a maze of the most confusing kind.

"Who are you?" Brene eventually asked.

The man spoke loudly, his deep voice echoing in the air around. "You may call me Zak," the man said with an air of importance. "For now, that is all you must know until I am certain that you can be trusted."

"And if I can't be trusted?"

"Then, I'm afraid; you are of no use to me. I shall execute swiftly you and your friends. You have my word." The man tried to portray a character of honor, but Brene saw through his facade. "Here we are."

He stopped in front of a tent that stood out from the rest because of its deep red color.

Zak held the tent open for Brene and ushered her inside. Then he stuck his head in through the opening. "When you are ready, you may come back outside and tell me what you have decided." Then he released the entrance of the tent, remaining outside.

Brene looked around the inside of the tent, which was dark and uninviting. There was holes overhead that allowed a few beams of moonlight to enter, which served as the only source of light. The ground was covered in hay and mud. On either side of her, large cages made of metal bars as thick as her arms.

"Brene?" Moria's voice was soft and shaky.

"Moria." She rushed to the cage from which she heard Moria's voice and dropped to her knees. She reached her hand into the cage and took Moria's hand. "Are you okay?"

Moria cried. "Ramdeo... Some of them were trying to touch me... They beat him," she shook her head. "He was too weak... he didn't have any power," Moria was whimpering now as she squeezed Brene's hands in hers.

"When was this?" Brene asked.

"Last night. I didn't see him today," Moria sniffled.

"It's okay. I saw him earlier today. He's alive."

Moria breathed in profoundly and whimpered out a sigh. "Are you sure?"

Brene nodded, and Moria released her hands to wipe her face.

"Moria, where are we?"

Moria took a few moments to catch her breath before

speaking. "I don't know where we are exactly," she shook her head. "But the man. The one with the dark hair and the ring..," Moria grabbed the bars and pulled herself close so that Brene could hear her. Brene saw her knuckles were covered in blood. "He's the Cursed One, Brene."

Brene felt her hands grow sweaty as she listened to Moria.

"And he believes that you're the Pure Bride," Moria said in almost a whisper.

"Me? Why?" Brene could hear, once again, that her voice was shaky.

Moria looked down and shook her head before rubbing her nose with the back of her hand and looking up again. "Because you are," Moria held her gaze. "The Supreme Pagzmans have been keeping tabs on you for years. When you were orphaned as a child, they placed you in a home that they had easy access to, but when the Caeruleus had found out about your powers, and you fled your Village, they felt like they had lost control. So, they invited you to work with us." Moria's eyes welled with tears once again. "I didn't know. I swear I didn't, Brene. They just told us you were important. But then, I read the map, and I had all those visions." She looked down again and closed her eyes tightly. "When Pannosus comes of age, there's a power signature sent out into the universe." Moria lifted her head again. "Few people know about it, but Aligists can read them, like a language. Yours was the most powerful the Supreme Pagzmans have seen in centuries."

Brene stared at Moria, not quite knowing what to feel.

"Your hands," she began. "Why haven't you healed them?"

Moria shook her head.

"I don't have the power," Moria wiggled her legs, and Brene heard the familiar sound of heavy metal chains. "They have some sort of jinx on them."

"I'm going to get us out of here, Moria. Where are the others?"

"They're in a similar tent on the other side of the camp. The men here forced them to work during the day."

"Okay—"

"Brene. The man. The Cursed One. Layton said there's something dark about him. He said he saw him kill a man by the touch of his hand."

Brene's eyes welled with tears at how helpless she felt. She dropped her head forward to rest on the metal bars and allowed the tears to flow.

Moria placed her hand under Brene's chin in a motherly way and forced her to look into her eyes. "You're going to be alright," Moria smiled, and Brene felt a warm boost of energy from Moria's faith in her. "You need to find Layton." eyebrows raised, Moria nodded slowly.

Brene returned the nod. "I won't leave you behind."

"I know. I'm the backbone of this team."

The two girls giggled, and then Brene reluctantly stood to leave. She turned back and smiled at Moria one last time before exiting the tent and feeling the shock of the ice-cold air outside.

"Ready to talk?" Zak asked. He was sitting on a barrel a few feet away from the tent, carving a piece of wood with a small dagger.

"Are you ready to tell me the entire story?" Brene asked; her courage now almost completely restored.

CHAPTER 16

BRENE SAT in the large armchair opposite Zak and waited patiently for him to talk. The man seemed to study her, every so often smiling to himself as though it satisfied him with what he found. Brene scowled at the man and narrowed her eyes.

"You are strong," Zak said, and nodded in approval. "But you are scared." He stopped nodding, and his face took up a countenance of seriousness.

"Who are you, exactly?" Brene asked, brushing his comments aside.

"Do you know the lore of the Myxan?" he asked.

Brene shrugged her shoulders. "Enlighten me."

He studied her for a moment longer before he told his tale.

"At the beginning of time," he spoke with an air of importance, "there was nothing. Until creatures of all kinds appeared on the land. Some creatures took it upon themselves to build a great wall, dividing the lands into north and south," he paused to ensure she understood. "In the North, the non-magical people surfaced, and they shared the lands with shape-shifters and other creatures who had known little but strife and hardships. The humans hunted them, forced to live in the shadows, and never truly felt safe." Zak reached into his shirt and pulled out a necklace, the pendant of which was the head of a leopard.

"One day, the great shape-shifter leaped over the wall and had a taste of the Southern lands," he hissed, disdain in his voice. "There, he saw no suffering or pain. The people there were Pannosus, and so they shared the lands equally with the other magical creatures. They lived happily and in peace, and the shape-shifter craved that kind of safety."

He tucked the pendant back into his shirt.

"At the time," he continued, "the shape-shifter was in love with one of his own. A beautiful woman, as pure as the light of day, who could change, at will, into any bird of flight. But his family disapproved of her, for they saw she was not pure. She had loved another before him and had born that man a baby. But the child was killed by its father, as often happened in the Northern lands.

"After the shape-shifter had experienced the joy of life in the south, however, the southerners raised the wall. Preventing any others from jumping over and disturbing the balance of the world. This enraged the shape-shifter, for he felt the Pannosus selfish and cruel that they did not allow him to be part of their world. He could not understand how they lived so peacefully when such unspeakable acts were committed among their kin in the Northern lands. For all those with magic running through their veins must be connected, after all."

Zak paused once again.

"The shape-shifter became enraged by the injustice, and so, the first life he took was that of a farm boy. He took the boy's life in the shape of a man, but somehow, it fueled the leopard side of him. He became stronger, faster, and larger.

He had never taken the life of an innocent before. Somehow, the boy's soul became a part of his own and gave him strength and courage beyond compare. Then, an idea came to him," Zak spoke proudly now.

"He had watched the southerners heal with their magic, and so he healed humans with his own power, but in return, they were to bind their souls to his. Their souls would power him, and if need be, they could harness a small amount of his own power for their use.

"In this way, the great shape-shifter recruited thousands of men and women alike, and they took the wall, invading the south. Alas, a band of witches and warlocks had devised a plan to trap the great beast in a bejeweled mercury box. But his spirit was too powerful, and so the great shape-shifter became the box in which he was imprisoned, waiting patiently for his salvation.

"His lover, who fought beside him in the battle, and who he swore would be his only bride, was banished to the great canyon that cuts through the Mendi Mountains. Discovering that the great beast lived on in the Myxan, the wizards and warlocks who formed the first ten members of the Order cast a spell that would soon turn into prophecy."

Zak got up from his chair and paced the floor.

"The power that the Myxan held was insurmountable, and so the release of that power was inevitable. So, the Order made it so that for the power of the Myxan to be unleashed, the great shape-shifter must come to power and consummate his marriage with a Pure Bride. Knowing that the love that the shape-shifter had for his Lady Paola was far too great to betray, the Order felt comfort in their spell.

"So, the Lady Paola spends her days taking the souls of the pure, hoping if she consumes enough, she will release her love," Zak returned to his seat and looked deep into Brene's eyes, smiling a cold and unsettling smile.

"I was the one who grabbed the Myxan from the pedestal in The War of the Ancestors." He allowed that fact to sink in.

Brene tried to hide her surprise but feared that it was painted plain on her face.

"I was told not to let the box touch my skin, but I did. And this appeared," he held out his right hand and showed Brene his palm, where the same symbol as his ring was imprinted. It looked to be engraved into his flesh, the symbol appearing as deep indentations in his palm. "Then, a couple days later, the voice spoke to me. It was the great shape-shifter himself. He said he was tired and ready to go, and he wanted me to have his power. He saw in my soul that I was worthy," Zak smirked, his countenance showing how proud he was of himself.

"And so he gave me his power. When the Order cast that spell all those years ago, they assumed that the Cursed One would be the shape-shifter himself. And that the impossibility of his Pure Bride would keep the world safe. But they were wrong."

Zak shifted his body to sit on the edge of his seat and leaned towards Brene.

"You are my Pure Bride, Brenley. You're the most powerful Pannosus to be born in the last 300 years. Merge our bond," he urged. "Gift me your virginity and join me in righting the wrongs of the world. Help me bring justice to this unjust world."

Brene looked at him blankly and opened her mouth to speak, but Zak continued.

"The blood moon is a fortnight away. We must marry and consummate our bond," he reached out and grabbed her hands. "We will be all-powerful together. I can teach you so much." He nodded enthusiastically.

Brene pulled her hands back and held them close to her chest, turning her eyes away from him and looking down.

"I see," Zak stood abruptly, rage in his eyes at her rejection. "Let me be very clear, Brenley. I can wait another 300 years for another Pure Bride. But your friends will not see the morning light."

Brene stood suddenly, tears in her eyes, and looked deep into Zak's eyes. Then she muttered. "What do I need to do?"

"Glad to see you've come to your senses." He smiled and took her hand, and then he led her outside the tent where there was still a business about. The men and women dropped to their knees and bowed, but before they could chant, Zak's voice echoed through the camp. "The Pure Bride has agreed to our cause!"

The men and women cheered happily, some hugging each other in celebration and others bumping their cups of ale together. Then Zak led her back into the tent.

"You may stay here until we are married." He nodded, then turned to leave the tent, but before he could exit, he turned back to face Brene one more time. "If I hear that you have tried to escape, your friends will be tortured. And I will make you watch."

With that, he left, leaving Brene alone with her thoughts.

For a moment, Brene stood in silence, a numbness washing over her. Then, she fell to the ground near where Ramdeo had bled earlier and cried, feeling helpless and alone. She laid there on the floor, hugging her knees into her chest, and gently rocking her body.

CHAPTER 17

A LOUD TRUMPET caused Brene to wake with a shock. She found herself on the floor where she had laid down the night before, still hugging her knees tightly. She released her knees and stretched her body before getting up off the floor and wiping the sleep out of her eyes. Her body ached all over, and her head was pounding from the lack of sleep and hunger alike. A second trumpet sounded, and Brene exited the tent to see what the commotion was about outside.

The daylight struck her almost violently, and she quickly brought her hands to her eyes to allow them to adjust. She heard the heaving, breathing and grunting of horses. So she followed the sound to a stable nearby, where Zak was mounting his horse and calling orders to those around him.

"Ah, my bride," he said in Brene's presence. "I must travel to a few villages further East through the mountains to recruit more members for our cause. The more souls we have, the more powerful we can become." He smirked, and the surrounding men cheered. "I will be back before the blood moon." He nodded at her. "In the meantime, learn our ways well. People do not trust a leader who is unlearned in their ways." His tone was stern, with a hint of warning underneath his words.

Brene nodded slowly, a sense of numbness still lingering in her body and mind.

"My friends," Brene shouted. "Will they be alright?"

"I have instructed my men not to harm them," he said. The irritation in his voice at the mention of her friends was clear. "Do not waste your time with concern for them. You must learn to lead our people."

With that, Zak held on tight to the horse's reins. He led a group of men out of the stables and towards the open land on the far side of the camp.

Brene watched quietly as the horses galloped away, then turned around and scanned the area for a way back to her tent.

"Let me show you, my lady," a young woman, not much older than Brene herself, approached her and smiled kindly. "I was quite confused when I first came here as well."

She pointed down to the ground at pebbles laid in long straight lines, creating pathways around the camp.

"Thank you, um...."

"Greta, my lady," she bowed her head slightly. "It's an honor to make your acquaintance."

"Thank you, Greta," Brene forced a smile. "Do you know where I could get something to eat?"

* * *

AFTER GRETA HAD INSISTED on drawing Brene a bath, the young girl took it unto herself to prepare a feast of chicken broth, bread rolls, fruits, and vegetables. Which she laid out on a medium-sized table in the corner of Brene's tent.

"I've boiled the water and positioned the bath behind your tent, my lady. Don't worry; nobody goes near there, so not a soul will see you." Great smiled proudly. "I've also brought some clean clothes. They're nothing fancy, but—"

"They're perfect, Greta. Thank you." Brene gratefully took the clothes that Greta handed her, all the while wondering how such a thoughtful young woman involved herself with such an awful cause.

When Greta left the tent, Brene ate to her heart's content, stuffing her face with bread rolls and chicken broth. Then she took off her clothes and placed them neatly on the bed before washing herself and putting on the clothes that Greta had so graciously gifted her. She pulled on a pair of brown cargo pants and a black long sleeve shirt, and then she laced up her boots. She grabbed a couple of apples and wrapped them in her old shirt, and then she tied it up like a knapsack, creating a sling which she slid her arm through.

She combed through the tent for any sort of weapon she could use. When she found none, she gave up completely, exiting the tent feeling a little defeated.

What did you think, Brene? Zak was just going to leave you a weapon to overthrow him? Grow up! She berated herself in her head.

As she stepped outside her tent, the people around stopped and bowed, cheering in unison, "Hail the Pure Bride!"

The sudden uproar startled Brene greatly, and so she decided it was time for her first address to her people. She found a barrel nearby and lifted herself up to stand on it. Then she cleared her throat and began to speak loudly.

"My people," she spoke. "It is true, I am the Pure Bride." She watched the people's eyes light up as they listened attentively to her speak. "But we all stand for the same cause. Please, do not think of me any greater than you or your brothers or your sisters. We are all the same." The people cheered happily. "My dream is your dream." They clapped at her words. "And we shall realize soon our dreams."

There was a loud uproar of applause, and two men stepped forward to help Brene down from the barrel. She smiled at one man, a middle-aged man holding a hammer, and asked him kindly where she could find the slaves.

"I was instructed by the Cursed One to cast my magic on them," she explained. "But this place is such a maze."

Brene forced a laugh and touched the man's arm, creating a sense of camaraderie between them, and the man happily showed her the way.

On the other side of the camp was an extensive excavation in which dozens of men were carrying large rocks on their backs, wearing nothing but their underwear. Brene stood atop a hill and watched the men, wondering what the purpose of the exercise was at all. Three men with whips walked around the excavation slowly, shouting orders at the slaves with the threat of their wrath.

Brene slowly made her way down the hill and approached the man with a whip. "Excuse me?"

The man's eyes widened and he bowed his head swiftly. "My lady, what an honor. How may I be of service?"

"The men and woman that I arrived with. The Cursed One has instructed that I cast my magic on them, forcing them to turn to our side. Where are they?" She forced a cunning smile.

The man studied her curiously before speaking again. "The master has not informed me of such a plan. They have been scheduled to the excavation site on the other side of the river," he said, narrowing his eyes. "What kind of magic are you to perform?"

Brene felt the sweat accumulate in her palms as she tightened her fists, forcing herself to remain calm.

"Glad you asked," she replied. "I'm also going to need thirteen animals. A variety of hooved animals and winged animals will do. If you find any babies, that would be great," she chuckled. "I find that Nedeaubre magic works better when you sacrifice baby animals." She shrugged.

The man's mouth curled into a big smile.

"Alright, my lady," he nodded. "I will have the imposters sent to your tent."

"Good. And one more thing," the relief that Brene felt was giving her more confidence by the second. "Have someone move four cages into my tent. The spells may take a few days, and I can't have them living like us." She shook her head, trying hard to create an air of importance to herself. "And the Cursed One shall know how helpful you have been... Um..."

"Oh, Casen, my lady," he bowed once again. "The name's Casen."

"Casen," Brene nodded and smiled, and then she turned her attention to the excavation. "Excellent job. Are we any closer?" Brene knew she was pushing her luck, but she needed to get as much information as possible.

"We'll find it, my lady, don't worry. We have eight dig sites in the area. I'm certain that the mercury box is in one of them. Just the other day, we cast another spell to narrow down the search. It's in the area, my lady, I'm sure of it."

The Myxan? What did Zak need the Myxan for if he had all the power of the great shape-shifter like he had said?

"Good work," Brene smiled, and then she turned around and made her way back to her tent.

By the time Brene had reached her tent, which was quite a distance away from the end of the camp, even without the roundabout way that she took, the cages she had requested had already been installed. She brushed her fingers against the cold steel of the bars, and then let her head rest against them, thinking hard about what her next move was going to be.

"My lady."

She turned around at the sound of a man's voice in her tent. Before her were Ishaan, Ramdeo, and Layton, all stripped down to their underwear with shackles around their wrists and ankles.

"These are the slaves you requested," Casen had delivered them himself.

"Very good." It took Brene every fiber of self-control in her body to maintain her air of indifference at the sight of her friends. "Put them in the cages. I cannot touch them until I have completed five sacrifices."

"Yes, my lady. The girl is being brought by Greta. She is very fond of you, my lady," Casen smiled proudly.

"And I of her, Casen."

The sound of his name made Casen's face turn red, and he hurriedly excused himself after placing the three men in the cages. All the while, the men looked at Brene with confusion washed over their faces, unable to speak.

Shortly after that, Greta entered the tent with Moria and a box of ducklings. She placed Moria in the cage as instructed and the box on the floor near Brene's bed.

"I am not to be disturbed," Brene said authority in her voice. "If one of my spells is not completed properly, I'm afraid my life may be altered."

Greta gasped at the notion and nodded vigorously.

"I will place a spell on the entrance of my tent to protect my life and those around me," Brene forced a smile as Greta turned around and left.

Brene stood silently, breathing loudly and allowing her heart rate to return to normal. Ishaan, Ramdeo, and Layton all stood with their hands against the metal bars, and Moria reached over to touch Ramdeo's arm through the partition in the cage. Nobody dared to say anything for a long time.

Brene moved towards the tent entrance and listened carefully for any movement outside, then pointed her arms toward a set of bookshelves. The bookshelves became encapsulated in a bright green bubble and floated up into the air. Brene moved her arms slowly, swiveling her body around, the bookshelves moving with her arms. Then she slowly lowered the bookshelves in front of the tent entrance, covering the slit completely.

She sighed out loud and leaned against the table, dropping her head down and closing her eyes. She lifted her right hand and pinched the bridge of her nose. Suddenly, she lifted her head and hurried to the cages, where her friends stood silently watching her.

"Oh, fuck! I'm so sorry," she apologized as she opened the cages.

The five of them chuckled, embracing each other hard and holding on for longer than necessary.

"I thought you had flipped your switch there, to be honest," Ishaan said to Brene, and they all laughed a little harder.

"Now what?" Ramdeo asked. His face and mouth looked to be slightly healed.

"Now, we train," Layton said, a wide, knowing smile painted on his face.

* * *

THE GROUP SLEPT PEACEFULLY that night, separated from the rest of the world outside. When morning had come, Layton woke to find Brene already up, sitting deep in thought in the middle of the room.

"Thanks for saving us," he whispered, moving a little closer to Brene. He smiled when Brene met his gaze.

"We need to get those chains off," Brene sounded worried.

Layton nodded. "And you're scared you'll drain someone."

The silence that followed was piercing.

"I won't let that happen," Layton's words caused a warmth to move through Brene's body. A feeling of comfort searing through her being. Somehow, with him there, she knew in her heart that it would all be alright.

Brene nodded.

"Who did that to Ramdeo?" she asked, nodding in his direction.

"Casen," Layton said in an unforgiving tone in his voice.

"Casen, it is," Brene held his gaze.

Brene moved the shelf away from the tent entrance then went outside and announced that she would like to see Casen. In about half an hour, the man entered the tent, a look of excitement and pride on his face. The Verdigris were standing inside their cages, their hands against the bars.

"Unconscious only," Brene said out loud.

"I beg your—"

Brene placed her hands around Casen's wrist, feeling the power surge through her. Her eyes glowed a bright shade of green, the same as her hands, and Casen struggled to breathe. Layton pushed open his cage and stood next to Brene, and the others followed suit.

"Only take as much as you need, Brene," Layton said, his voice soothing and calm. But it was no use. Before he could speak again, Casen's lifeless corpse lay on the ground, and Brene heard nothing but a buzzing in her ears.

"She's taking too much," Ishaan said.

Layton wrapped his chains around Brene's hands, and they burst to pieces from her power. Then, he pulled the rest of them forward and did the same, but Brene didn't power down.

"She's taken too much," Moria said, concerned.

Layton pulled Brene close and kissed her hard, absorbing the excess power from within her. As they kissed, the bright green light that had consumed Brene's body faded until it had altogether disappeared. Brene pulled away from Layton and looked down at Casen's lifeless body, and then she buried her face in Layton's chest and wept.

CHAPTER 18

"I CAN'T DO IT," Brene mumbled as she wept into Layton's chest. "I drained him. I wasn't even in control of my senses. The power is too much."

Layton placed his hands on her shoulders and pushed her gently away so that he could look into her eyes. He lifted his hand and pushed a curl of her hair away from her face. "You just need a little practice, Brene. You can do this."

Brene wiped her face with the back of her hands and pulled her nose in. Then she looked at the others who were rubbing their wrists, grateful that their shackles had been broken. Ramdeo grabbed Moria, and the two embraced for a long time before turning back to the group to devise a plan.

"Thank you, Brene," Ishaan said and patted her on the shoulder with care.

"You can thank me when we're out of here." She smiled and chuckled, then rubbed her puffy eyes. "So, what's the plan? Zak said he'd be back by the blood moon. That's in just over ten days, I think."

"For now, like I said, we train." Layton looked at the others.

"What did you tell them about us?" Ramdeo asked. "How did you convince them to let us stay here?"

"I told them that Zak told me to cast spells on you so that you come onto our side."

Moria nodded. "Brilliant. Tomorrow, go outside and tell them that the spells are cast, but it came at a cost, and Casen volunteered for the great sacrifice."

Brene felt a knot in her stomach at the mention of Casen, and she dropped her gaze to the ground. Then, she remembered how Ramdeo looked when they arrived, and a fire brewed inside her. She nodded and looked up.

"Inform your followers that we, Moria, Ramdeo, and I, will overlook serious tasks in the camp," Ishaan said. "I'll order a team to remove Casen's body and the cages and put up two tents adjoining yours."

"And I," Layton said, smiling, "will train you, young Ipian."

Brene felt a familiar warmth engulf her once again, and she smiled happily at spending more time with Layton. She nodded.

They spent the rest of the day planning the attack on Zak and his army of men, all of whom had pledged their loyalty and souls to his cause. Then, by nightfall, there was a ruffling at the entrance of the tent.

"My lady?" Greta called through the slit. "I have brought you some fresh food."

"Enter," Brene said; the conviction in her tone.

Greta entered the tent carrying a large pot of stew and two loaves of freshly baked bread. She laid them on the table and screamed in horror as her eyes fell on Casen's drained corpse.

Brene maintained her air of indifference and royalty. She slowly walked to Greta and placed her hands gently on her shoulders.

"The imposters have been broken," she whispered softly.

"Casen knew the importance of his sacrifice. When I requested he bring me another slave to drain their power, he said that he would be honored if I used him instead."

Greta cried and held her hand against her mouth, her body shaking as she whimpered.

"He was brave," she said proudly, smiling through her tears. Then she lifted her head and studied the others hard. "Can they hear me?" she whispered to Brene.

"They can hear you, yes. But they listen only to me and the Cursed One," Brene forced a smile.

And just like that, the first part of the plan was already in motion.

* * *

"THE KEY to controlling your magic is not focus or concentration." Layton shook his head as he wrapped a piece of cloth around his fists. "It's knowing who you are."

Brene looked at him, feeling more confused than ever.

"What kind of bullshit lesson is this?" she asked; irritation in her voice.

Layton chuckled at her response and continued. "The problem with you is that you're too focused on what you're doing and not why you're doing it."

Brene grunted. They had walked almost two hours to get to the riverside, far enough away so that Zak's men could not see or hear them. Her legs were throbbing, and she was sweating profusely in the heat of the day.

Layton raised his eyebrows and stared at her down.

"Fine. Go on. I'm listening."

"Come at me," Layton said, smirking.

"What?"

"Come at me." He stretched out his hands in a fighting stance and widened his legs for anchorage.

Brene ran towards him at full force, punching fast, but missing every shot. Layton moved swiftly and gracefully, an incandescent orange light following the path that his body took.

"That's not fair. You're using your powers." Brene stood, breathing heavily.

"Exactly, Brene!" Layton said earnestly. "You should use yours too. We're not fighting local thugs at the bar," his tone was serious. "What are you so afraid of? So, you drained a couple of people. That doesn't make you a bad person," he was talking loudly.

"I know that!" Brene shouted.

"I don't think you do!" Layton matched her volume. He sighed loudly, and then began to speak softly. "I'm sorry. I just..," he shrugged. "I don't understand why you're so scared."

Brene stood quietly and shifted her gaze to the river.

"The power," she began. "It's too much." She wrapped her arms around herself, hugging her body protectively. "You asked how it felt. The first time I drained someone," her voice sounded shaky, like she was fighting back the tears. "It felt glorious. I didn't care about his family or his life. All I could think about was the power entering my body."

"Good," Layton said.

Brene turned around and gave him a dangerous look.

"Good?" she spat.

"You're finally honest with yourself," Layton smiled, ignoring the fury on Brene's face. "That's a good start."

He scanned the area and found two large sticks on the ground that had fallen from a nearby tree. He threw one to Brene and held one in his own hands like a weapon.

"The power feels glorious. You said it yourself. So, to counteract the high that you get when you absorb power from another, ground yourself."

Brene widened her stance for balance.

"Not in your stance," Layton smirked and shook his head. "Inside you." He walked towards Brene and held out his stick like a sword. "What do you stand for?" His stick glowed orange.

"I don't know," Brene looked at her stick, which was still its dull brown color.

"Come on, Brene. What's important enough that you would die for it?" Layton's stick glowed brighter.

"I don't know," she was getting frustrated now.

"When you saved Moria in the canyon. What was going through your mind then?" His stick glowed brighter still.

"I didn't want her to get hurt," Brene said softly, and to her surprise, her stick glowed a dull hue of green. Her eyes widened in excitement, and her mouth widened into a smile.

"Why not?" Layton asked, smiling to himself.

"I don't know," Brene said, and just like that, her stick returned to its original dull color.

"Don't focus! Don't think! Just feel!" Layton urged. "Why didn't you want Moria to get hurt?"

"Because I had finally found a friend in her!" Brene shouted, louder than necessary, and her stick ignited into green flames. She dropped it to the ground and screamed loudly, then dropped to her knees and hung her head low.

Layton dropped his stick and made his way to her. Next, he fell to the floor next to her and took her hand.

"That's progress," he smiled. "The hardest part is over."

They threw their bodies back onto the soft grass and laid there, staring up at the fluffy white clouds in the bright blue sky.

"Do you know how rare Ipians are?" Layton asked as they laid there. Brene continued to stare at the sky. "The lore says that one is born for every 500 million Pannosus. In one generation, there are only five or six, and the record for the largest number of Ipian to exist on Earth at the same time was sixteen. Can you imagine? Only sixteen of our kind existed at a time, and that was the maximum?"

"Did you learn from an Ipian? How to control your powers, I mean," Brene turned her head toward him.

Layton breathed in heavily and sighed out. Then he turned his head toward her. "I wasn't completely truthful about how I came to live with the Verdigris."

Brene sat up and turned her body towards him, listening attentively. Layton sat up slowly.

"I was born a Caeruleus."

Shock washed over Brene's body, but she continued to focus.

"My mother died in childbirth, and after that, my father didn't want me anymore. The midwife who helped deliver me possessed great power, and she told my father that I would grow to become an Ipian. Naturally, my father planned to sacrifice me for my power."

Brene gasped loudly.

"Anyway, the midwife worked for some of the royalty among the Caeruleus. The night before the ritual in which I was to be sacrificed, she stole me away and brought me to the Caeruleus palace. In Prague."

"Prague? The Marauder Queen?" Brene whispered.

Layton nodded. "The Marauder queen adopted me. She taught me all that I know. But she was evil and unforgiving. She cast torturous spells on her children, claiming she was making us strong. I would sleep in the dungeons, and every so often, she would send down someone who had wronged her, and I would drain them of their life."

Brene lifted her hand to her mouth in horror, and she watched Layton's eyes closely. She saw sadness and longing in them.

"But it wasn't all that bad," Layton smiled to himself.

"There was a cook who I loved like a mother. She would sneak down into the dungeons and bring me cakes and biscuits when nobody was around. She would tell me stories and make me laugh."

He looked over Brene's shoulder longingly, allowing his mind to wander.

"She loved me dearly, as I did her," he paused. "The Marauder queen killed her."

Brene saw a tear fall down his cheek.

"Anyway..." He wiped the tear away. "Ishaan found me on the streets when I was about sixteen. We bonded almost immediately," he smiled.

"What was her name?" Brene asked softly. "The cook?"

Layton smiled, "Alexandria." He stood up and dusting the grass off his bottom. "And she is what kept me grounded."

Brene followed suit. "I don't have any family."

"But you long for a connection. That's why your power was so strong when you saved Moria. You care for her."

Brene thought for a long moment.

"You need to find something you care about. Something that makes you feel happy and whole. Use it to ground you," Layton picked up another two sticks and threw one to Brene. "Ready."

Brene felt a little more confident now.

"Ready," she smirked.

CHAPTER 19

FOR THE NEXT WEEK, Brene and Layton trained almost all day, every day. She graduated from fighting with sticks and twigs to fully blown blades that glowed bright green under her control. She had found her grounding. It was the same as Layton's. It was the people that she loved and cared for. She no longer felt fear or uncertainty, only courage and determination.

Her combat skills had grown to become refined and well-executed. She moved as swiftly and gracefully as a swan and as intentionally as an assassin.

"Alright," Layton said. "Get into the water."

"What?"

"Get. Into. The. Water," Layton said slowly.

"You're kidding," Brene scrunched her eyebrows together.

"Do I sound like I'm kidding?" Layton smirked.

The two climbed into the river and made their way towards the middle of the gently flowing current.

"Water is a universal conductor. That means magic too," Layton explained. "There's water in the air, in the ground, even in our bodies. So, use it. Lift me up."

Brene stared at Layton blankly. "Um…"

"Lift me up out of the water and drop me on the land."

"Layton, I don't think—"

"Feel the water around you. Allow your power to flow through it and then further through the water in my body. You can do it." Layton floated further away from Brene until the sound of the river muffled his voice flowing. "Come on! I don't have all day."

Brene took a deep breath in and looked in Layton's direction. She felt the water flowing around her body and cast out her power so that it glowed bright green around her. Then she allowed the water to carry her magic towards Layton, the green light from her body flowing against the current.

"That's it!" Layton shouted.

Soon, the light had surrounded Layton completely, creating a capsule around him, and lifted his body into the air. The water dripped down from his soaked clothes back into the river as she screamed in excitement, like a child on a rollercoaster. Brene smiled at the sound of his enthusiasm. Then, the bright green bubble in which Layton was floating moved over to the river's side and descended to the ground, just in front of a large tree.

Layton landed on his feet and threw his arms in the air, jumping up and down like a child. "Yes! You did it!"

Brene laughed and splashed around in the water, screaming happily. Then she swam to the river bank, pulled her body out, and ran to Layton, jumping into his arms and gripping him. Layton spun her around, giggling happily, before pulling his face away slightly and looking deep into Brene's eyes.

Brene saw his eyes dart down to her lips, and without thinking, she leaned into him, pressing her mouth against his. She moved her hands against his skin from the back of his neck, down into his soaked shirt, and kissed him hard.

When she finally released his lips, she held her face against his cheek that was cold from the river, closing her eyes and feeling his presence.

"You should probably get those clothes off," she whispered. "I'd hate for you to get a cold."

Layton giggled as he rubbed his face against hers. Brene reached her hands underneath his shirt and pulled it off over his head, and then she took off hers as well.

"Brene—"

"Shh," Brene kissed him again, pressing her body against his.

Layton lifted her up, throwing her legs around his waist, and pressed her up against the tree. He gently kissed her neck, and then playfully grabbed her breast, stroking her nipple. Then he reached down and unbuttoned her pants with one of his hands. He slipped his hand inside her pants and gently massaged the flesh in between her legs, causing Brene to gasp and moan in pleasure.

* * *

MORIA HURRIEDLY MADE her way to Ramdeo, who was overseeing the blacksmith's duties and weapons' production. She hurried into the tent and then took a deep breath in before speaking.

"Ramdeo," she said in an indifferent tone, as though she was not entirely in her senses. "The Pure Bride wishes to see us in her tent."

She nodded at her husband and left the tent slowly, then waited outside for him to follow.

When Ramdeo exited the tent, Moria grabbed him frantically and pulled him aside, leading him behind the tent. Then she looked around to ensure no one was listening before grabbing his collar and looking deep into his eyes. "Zak is back." There was panic in her voice.

* * *

BRENE AND LAYTON were naked on the soft grass now. The warmth of Layton's body on top of hers made her feel safe. Layton kissed her neck and crept down her body. He took her nipple in his mouth, moaning as he played with it with his teeth. Then, he spread her legs, caressing her wet flesh with his tongue and forcing her back to arch as pleasure jolted through her body. Brene ran her fingers through his thick, rough hair as she moaned.

Layton lifted his head and shifted his body, positioning himself so that his face was now close to Brene's again. He looked deep into her eyes and smiled. Brene saw his eyes well with tears as he looked at her. Then he entered her, causing her to gasp once again, slowly moving in and out.

"Are you alright?" he breathed.

Brene nodded, her eyes closed all the while.

"We can stop—"

"Don't stop, Layton," Brene panted, "Please, don't stop." She dug her fingers into his back, pulling him closer to her.

* * *

MORIA AND RAMDEO moved quickly through the camp, looking frantically for Ishaan.

"Where is he?" Ramdeo was worrying.

* * *

BRENE WAS LYING in Layton's arms on the soft grass where they had just made love, their naked bodies covered only with his shirt, which was still slightly damp. Brene could still feel a beating in between her legs, and the heat from her loins had not yet gone. Her body was still tingling from Layton's touch.

Layton reached for her hand and interlaced his fingers in hers. "You know," he said, "According to the lore—"

"Where do you get all this lore from?" she teased.

"Hey! I like to read," he chuckled, playing with her fingers. "Anyway, as I was saying," He gave her a playful look. "According to the lore, Ipians are thought to belong in sets. And people believed that once two Ipians formed a set, they were bonded for the next seven lifetimes."

"Are you saying you want to be bonded to me for the next seven lifetimes?" Brene teased.

"Please, I don't even like you," Layton jokingly rolled his eyes. "But," he continued. "When an Ipian set had bonded, that the pair would become more powerful than ever. Each being able to feed off the others' energy without draining them."

Brene listened quietly, fantasizing about a life with Layton.

"We should get going now," he whispered. "I mean, I really don't want to."

Brene giggled.

"But I do believe there's some psychopath out there who wants to make you their bride soon, so..."

They reluctantly dressed, and Layton interlaced his fingers in Brene's as they made their way back to reality.

CHAPTER 20

As the campsite came into view, Brene released Layton's hand, and they shared a look. Then she walked ahead of him up the hill and towards her tent. All the while, she replayed the events of the day in her mind. Smiling to herself and holding her stomach, which felt as though butterflies were actively fluttering around in there.

Brene entered her tent, still smiling to herself, but then a panic jolted through her body that caused the color in her face to run.

"I'm back, my bride," Zak was grinning as he stood before her. In front of him, Moria, Ramdeo, and Ishaan were kneeling on the floor. Their hands shackled once again, each of them bleeding profusely from various puncture wounds in their abdomens. Ramdeo was coughing blood, and Ishaan's eyes were so swollen that she couldn't see whether or not they were open.

Brene heard the entrance of the tent flutter open, and a large, bald man pushed Layton forcefully past her and down to the ground next to the others. His hands were shackled as well, and there was blood dripping from over his left eyebrow.

Brene opened her mouth to speak, but somehow, she felt as though all the life she had left was drained from her body, and she was nothing more than an empty shell. She frantically scanned the faces of her friends before her. Hoping in her heart that they would give her some sort of sign to tell her what to do.

"Turns out, the blood moon is sooner than we expected," Zak continued to speak as he slowly paced behind her friends. "So, we shall begin the ceremony tonight. I have decided that these four will be the first to be sacrificed."

Brene fell to her knees, her mouth still open and her eyes filling with tears, all the while holding Layton's gaze, not noticing that Zak was studying her closely. Her mouth was still open, but her voice seemed not to be there.

"This one," he said to the bald man, nodding towards Layton. "Prepare him for the altar. He will be the one that my bride drains before we consummate our bond."

"No," Brene was shaking all over. "No. Please." She stood up and made her way to him, then put her palms together in a pleading motion.

Zak slapped her hard with the back of her hand, forcing her to fall to the ground.

As Brene fell to the ground, Layton screamed and leaped to his feet, tackling Zak and pushing him through the entrance of the tent and outside. The bald man pursued.

Brene got to her feet, her jaw tingling from the force of Zak's hand, and ran to Moria. She placed her hands on the shackles, trying hard to use her power to break them, but she could not. She was crying now and struggling to talk through her tears.

"Moria," she shook her head frantically. "I can't do it. I just can't do it."

"Brene!" Moria said sternly. "Listen to me carefully. Layton told me he taught you how you ground yourself. Right now, he's outside, getting beaten up by an all-powerful psychopath. We need to help him," she spoke quickly. "You can do it. Just breathe."

Brene breathed in deeply and nodded, and then she swallowed hard. She allowed her mind to wander back to the glorious day she had with Layton. She remembered how his body felt against hers when they moved in unison. How soft his lips were and how gently he caressed her. She remembered how loving his embraces felt and how much she had grown to care for him.

"That's it," Moria said excitedly.

Brene looked down to see that her hands were glowing brightly. She placed them on Moria's shackles, which immediately shattered, the pieces flying in all directions. Then, she did the same for Ramdeo and Ishaan before helping them to their feet and hugging them tightly. She healed her friends quickly and made sure they were alright before speaking.

"I've had enough of this. Let's get this guy and go home," Brene said confidently.

They hurried through the tent's exit and found that the men and women of the camp had gathered around, forming a large circle around Zak and Layton. Layton was on his knees, his face covered in blood, Zak throwing jinxes that shone a bright red color, like flashes of light soaring through the air.

Brene ran as fast as she could and placed her body between Layton and an incoming jinx. She lifted her arm, and a bubble encapsulated them, absorbing the jinx as it made contact. The red color disappeared among the bright green of Brene's power.

Zak watched Brene, his eyes growing wide with fury and anger. She turned around and broke Layton's shackles, then held his face in her hands. His face healed at her touch, and he smiled at her.

"Someone's mastered their powers," Layton whispered, and then he stood up, Brene rising next to him.

Zak laughed loudly and slowly circled the two. "Your power is no match for mine. I am the Cursed One." He continued to laugh. Then he conjured a ball of fire in his hands and released it toward the protective capsule in which Brene and Layton were standing. The green light of the capsule absorbed the fire quickly, never budging.

Zak's eyes opened wider, and he stopped in his tracks.

"Impossible," he whispered.

"Not impossible at all," Brene mocked him. The green light that encapsulated them disappeared. The others joined them in the middle of the clearing, all five facing Zak.

Zak swiftly conjured another ball of fire and released it in their direction. Brene moved quickly towards the ball, her hands glowing bright green, and simply caught it as though it were a basketball they were throwing among friends. She split the ball in her hand into many smaller balls and released them up into the air. When they fell back to the ground, they landed in all directions, setting many alight tents around the camp. Soon, the entire field was in flames, Zak's followers running in all directions trying to save their possessions.

"You see," Brene began, walking towards Zak slowly. "When I saw you had your men looking for the Myxan, I asked myself why? Why would the great Cursed One be looking for the Myxan if he had been gifted the magic of the great shapeshifter as he claimed? Then it hit me," she stopped walking. "You don't have the magic of the Myxan within you. You never did. Did you?"

The crowd gasped, and Zak's face fell.

"That's preposterous!" he spat.

"Oh? Don't you think the Cursed One could kill a few Verdigris?" Brene mocked him again, "Because we're all still here." She motioned back to her friends.

Brene saw the fury growing in Zak's eyes and expected another blow. He released a larger ball of fire in her direction, which she caught in her glowing hands once again, but this time squished between her palms into dust.

"You heard the voice after the insignia appeared on your hand, yes. I believe that. But you are not the Cursed One," Brene shook her head. "You are only his lap dog. His puppet that he urges to do his bidding until he is strong enough to rise once again." She laughed.

Zak leaped forward and grabbed Brene's arms, trying hard to drain her of power. But Brene simply stood there, holding his gaze as she felt his body buzz in effort. She leaned in towards him and whispered. "You know what you're missing? Grounding."

Brene placed her hands on Zak's wrists, and the man screamed in agony as she drained him of his power. Her eyes glowed a bright green that soon engulfed her whole body as Zak wasted away before her. Brene could feel the power inside her, flowing around so freely. She wanted more. She needed more. She needed to drain him.

Then, the image of Moria popped into her head. She was holding a map and smiling up at Brene. After that, Brene saw a vision of Ramdeo taking some of his rations and placing them on Brene's plate. Ishaan appeared in the scene and threw Brene a knife for her own protection. Last, Brene saw Layton in the middle of the river, cheering her on.

She released Zak's hands and stepped back.

The man before her looked thin and worn out, but he was alive and standing. Brene turned to his followers that had gathered around and spoke so loudly that her voice echoed through the camp. "You have been fed a lie, good people. This man is not the Cursed One. He is a fraud. He had been using you."

There was chatter and murmurs among the crowd.

"The Order is on their way," Brene continued. "They will surely want to speak to those who have disobeyed their laws in the name of power."

The crowd panicked and shuffled, screaming over each other as they moved.

"Pack up!" One man screamed.

"I'm too young to go to jail!" Another woman hurried away.

In the few moments that followed, Brene heard the sudden burst of many portals opening up around them, through which groups of people hurriedly jumped. Brene picked up a pair of shackles on the floor and put them around Zak's wrists. Then she handed the chains to Ramdeo, who smiled and nodded.

"So, who's the Cursed One then if this guy's just his puppet?" Moria asked Brene as they walked towards the forest on the side of the camp.

"I think it's the great shapeshifter," Brene said, sounding a little unconvinced.

"Wait, what? So, the prophecy says that the great shapeshifter is going to rise to power again?" Ishaan asked.

"Maybe. The Order should have more answers," Brene replied. "I figured the shapeshifter created a sort of bond with Zak when he touched the Myxan. So, he's been communicating with him all this time. If Zak had found the Myxan before the blood moon, he would have released the power of the great shapeshifter on the world.

"Any idea how to get back?" Ramdeo asked; pulling on the chain to force what was left of Zak to walk a little faster.

"I think I can find a way out," Moria said, looking around at the trees. She closed her eyes and bent down, placing her palms flat on the ground.

Layton walked up beside Brene and interlaced his fingers in hers with a smirk. "There's always Plan B."

ABOUT THE AUTHOR

Renee Joiner has been in love with the supernatural for longer than she can remember, so it is no surprise that she is an author of paranormal urban fantasy. Although she discovered her passion for writing when she was only twelve years old, she didn't make her writing debut until many years into the future. Adventurous and fun-loving, she enjoys traveling to new places, exploring new sights and meeting new people. Thus, she delights in creating fantastical worlds that are sure to give her readers an escape from the real world while simultaneously providing thrilling entertainment.

Besides her special knack for writing, you'll also find a passion for metaphysics spirituality which she has been nurturing for over four decades. Renee hails from New York and currently resides with her husband in their empty nest—unless you count their three adorable fur babies—in Florida. She enjoys adding to her sea of knowledge and thus spends her free time learning new things.

To find out more about Renee Joiner, feel free to visit her **official website.**

facebook.com/reneejoinerauthor
twitter.com/iamreneejoiner
instagram.com/reneejoinerauthor
amazon.com/author/reneejoiner

Thorne Sisters Chronicles
Possessed by Magic
Reincarnated by Magic
Immortal by Magic

SIGN UP TO RECEIVE MY NEWLETTER FOR ALL THE LATEST UPDATES AND SPECIALS!

RENEEJOINERAUTHOR.COM/NEWSLETTER

Thank You..

Thank you for reading my book!
I really appreciate all of your feedback and I love to hear what you have to say. Please leave your review at your favorite retailer!